5

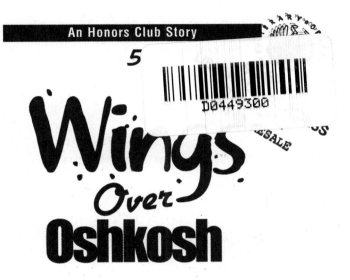

# Wings Over Oshkosh

## Charles Mills

**Pacific Press® Publishing Association**
Nampa, Idaho
Oshawa, Ontario, Canada
www.pacificpress.com

Designed by Tim Larson
Cover illustration © by Marcus Mashburn

Copyright 2005 by
Pacific Press® Publishing Association
Printed in United States of America

Additional copies of this book are available
by calling toll free 1-800-765-6955 or visiting
http://www.adventistbookcenter.com.

ISBN: 0-8163-2089-6

05 06 07 08 09 • 5 4 3 2 1

# Dedication

To my wife Dorinda,
the wings of all my dreams,
and to the awesome Pathfinders
at the Faith on Fire Camporee
who shared their ideas for this
and future Honors Club books.
You guys rule!

Other Honors Club books by Charles Mills

*The Bandit of Benson Park*
*Storm on Shadow Mountain*
*The Secret of Scarlett Cove*
*The Great Sleepy-Time Stew Rescue*

# Contents

# Chapter 1

# Light in the Sky

Jackie bent low over the handlebars and pedaled hard. She really didn't care where she was going—she just wanted to be somewhere else, somewhere away from the house on McCoy Street, away from the memories that haunted her every waking hour.

"It's not fair," she groaned through clenched teeth. "I didn't ask to be here. I didn't want to move so far away. And I certainly didn't plan to spend my life in a state with *no curves!*"

Jackie jammed on the brakes, skidded to a stop, and let the bicycle fall onto the shoulder of the road. Then she walked out to the centerline and stood staring down the highway that stretched away from her, arrow straight, into the gathering darkness. "What's wrong with you people?" she called, her words breathy and filled with frustration. "Haven't you ever heard of a curve? It goes like this." She made a swinging motion with her hand. "Does everything have to be so straight in this stupid state? Come on. Live a little. *Make a curve!*"

The only response she heard was the mournful cry of a screech owl floating out from a dark grove of trees off to her left.

Jackie sighed, letting her shoulders droop and her arms hang loosely at her sides. She stood motionless, listening to herself breathe, watching the silent march of night as it chased away the last dim light of dusk. One by one, stars sparkled on overhead, filling the sky with their cold, aloof presence. In all of her almost thirteen years, she'd never felt so alone, so cut off from everything she cared about and loved.

Slowly, she walked back to the edge of the highway and stood looking down at her fallen bike. She stared at it for a long moment, and then spoke quietly. "You can't take me home," she said, her words edged with deep sadness. "Nothing can."

As a familiar anger began to build inside her, Jackie pushed through the weeds and tall grasses growing beside the road and stumbled out onto a grassy field, where she walked aimlessly under the moonless sky. The air was cold, but she didn't care. Her slender body shivered beneath her thin blue jacket as she brushed auburn hair from her forehead and tried to see in the darkness with tear-filled eyes.

Reaching the far end of the expanse, she stopped and turned her face skyward. With fists gripped tightly at her sides, she shouted into the night air, "I hate You, God. I *hate* You!"

Suddenly, a soft glow began to illuminate her surroundings, revealing the outlines of small clumps of grass on the darkened surface of the field. The radiance grew more intense as a deep, throaty growl rose from somewhere in the stillness. Jackie stood motionless, her eyes opening wider and wider. Then the nearby trees began to take on silvery, ghostly shapes as rays of light slanted through their knotty branches and trembling leaves.

"What's happening?" Jackie gasped as she glanced first one way and then another, watching her world being transformed by some unseen, unknown brilliance.

The light grew brighter and brighter with each passing second. The sound that, at first, had been a throaty growl was quickly turning into a whistling, rumbling roar.

Jackie began to run on trembling legs, stumbling, tripping, blindly racing across the field. Glancing back over her shoulder, she saw two large, brilliant balls rise from the trees, pass over their tops, and then begin dropping in her direction.

"*No!*" she screamed. "*No, God!* I didn't mean it. *I didn't mean it!*"

Instantly, the lights and the roar were upon her. She flung herself hard to the ground, and her mouth filled with dirt and grass clippings as she pressed herself against the glowing surface of the field. She felt a great wind blow over her body, passing so violent that it rolled her over and over before letting her go. Then, all was quiet and dark save for a distant rumble and a low-voiced rush of air.

Jackie lay on the ground, her breath coming in quick, violent gasps. Had God Himself come down to punish her for her bold, angry statement? Was her life now ending on this flat, deserted field? She lay where the rushing wind had deposited her, afraid to move, afraid of what she might see if she opened her eyes and lifted her head.

When a few moments had passed, she heard the growl returning, this time slowly, deliberately. A quick peek through one slightly opened eye revealed that, as she feared, a powerful beam was lighting the ground once again. But this time, the sound hesitated some distance away and stayed relatively low, as if some unknown creature was waiting, watching, expecting her to do something.

Hesitantly, she opened both eyes and lifted herself up on one elbow. Far down the field, two brilliant lights were hovering above the ground. Slowly, she rose to her feet and faced the roaring beast.

The two stood staring at each other for a long moment. Then, with a blast of air and an angry roar, the attacker turned, revealing its true identity. It was a twin-engine aircraft sitting high on strong steel legs, rolling on feet made of rubber. The plane taxied away, moving in the direction of a large barn guarding the edge of the forest that ran along one side of the broad field.

Jackie tried to regain her balance as she watched it go. The sight and sound of the powerful creature that, just moments ago, had almost ended her short life, sent shivers of both fear and fascination through her.

Pilot Sam Fieldstone pressed on the toe brakes as he eased the broad-winged Piper Aztec up to the front entrance of the barn that was his spacious hangar. He set the parking brake and pulled the mixture controls on the throttle quadrant to the full-lean position. The spinning propellers slowed as the air supply being fed to the inner workings of the two powerful engines was cut off. With a cough and shake, the aircraft became just another collection of metal and technology. Now it was incapable of flight, bound to the earth by the ever-present force of gravity. After switching off the taxi lights, radios, navigation instruments, and master electrical switch, the man sat unmoving in the cockpit, listening to the gyros slowly spin down and the muffled cracking and snapping of the engines as they cooled.

At this particular moment Sam felt old, much older than his sixty-eight years. Even though his usually unruly hair was mostly white, he had the burly build of a much younger man. His eyesight was still good, coordination topnotch, and he could handle an airplane as well as any fighter pilot. But he wasn't young, not anymore, and moments like this reminded him of that fact.

Sam climbed out of the aircraft and closed the door behind him. After stepping down from the wing, he was about to head into the barn to retrieve the small, motorized dolly he used to pull aircraft into his hangar when he heard someone speaking. "You almost killed me," a voice announced. Turning, he saw a girl standing at the tip of a wing.

"*You* almost killed *me*," he responded coldly. "I had to gun the engines just to make it over you." The man paused. "What were you doing out on my runway?"

"Runway?" Jackie gasped. "It's a field!"

Sam studied his visitor thoughtfully. Then he turned and headed once again for the hangar. "It's a runway, and you're trespassing," he called over his shoulder.

Jackie frowned. "You're not being very nice to me, seeing as you almost chopped me up with this . . . this . . . thing."

Sam chuckled. "This *thing* is a 1981 Piper Aztec, twin engine, IFR-equipped aircraft." He guided the dolly toward the front strut. "And what were you doing out there in the dark anyway? Aren't you supposed to be somewhere?"

"Not really."

Sam shook his head as he hooked the dolly to the front wheel and began carefully guiding the aircraft into the hangar. Once the big plane was in place, he unhooked the dolly and returned it to its spot by the wall. Then he walked to the front entrance and pressed a button, and a large door began to swing down from above. "Well, go back to wherever you're supposed to be and stay off my runway," he ordered into the darkness before retreating into the hangar as the door swung shut behind him, sealing out the night air.

"You're still not being very nice," a voice called from the other side of the Aztec. Sam gasped when he saw Jackie standing by his workbench, examining the collection of aircraft parts arranged neatly across its wooden surface. "What's this?" she asked, picking up what looked like a large chunk of metal. "It's heavy."

"Put that down!" Sam ordered as he hurried around the Aztec's tail and grabbed the item from his visitor's hands. "It's a cylinder head, and you're still trespassing. Except now you're trespassing in my hangar."

"Hangar?" Jackie laughed. "This is a barn."

"It's a hangar! Now, go away."

Jackie ambled over to another table, this one covered with electronic devices sporting strange-looking dials and colorful arrays of carefully crafted numbers. "Do you build airplanes?" she asked.

"I *fix* airplanes."

Jackie pointed at the Aztec. "That one broken?"

Sam sighed in frustration, not knowing what to do with the annoying stranger who refused to leave. "Not any more. I fixed it, OK? So, please get out of here."

"I live in West Virginia," Jackie said matter-of-factly, ignoring the command. "Well, at least I did. It's a beautiful state. Lots of mountains and *curves.*"

"Then go back to West Virginia."

"I can't. My mom and dad are in jail."

Sam blinked. "Both of them?"

"Yup. Dad for drug possession, and mom for stealing money from an insurance company. Don't get me wrong; they were great parents. We all got along just fine. But, as the pastor at my church told me, my parents made some pretty dumb choices."

Sam hesitated before speaking. "I . . . I'm sorry."

"Yeah, well, that's why I can't go back to West Virginia. Our house was sold to pay the insurance company. Is it fun to fly an airplane?"

Sam frowned and then nodded. "Yes. So, where are you living now?"

"In Lakeside. Just down the road . . . *straight* down the road. Have you noticed that there aren't many curves in Wisconsin? Moved here 'bout a month ago. I live with my aunt, who thinks I'm . . . how did she put it this afternoon . . . 'worthless and a great burden.' Have you ever been to West Virginia?"

"No."

"Well, you should go there because it's beautiful. I lived in a town called Cyprus Hill. Had lots of friends." The girl paused, tilting her head slightly. "What's your name?"

"Sam. Sam Fieldstone. What's yours?"

"Jackie Anderson."

The old pilot cleared his throat. "Well, Jackie Anderson, I'm sorry that I frightened you out there on the fiel—ah, runway. I'm not used to having strange girls running around on my property."

Jackie chuckled. "Hey, I'm just glad it was you."

"What do you mean?"

She pointed toward the high ceiling of the hangar. "At first, I thought you were God," she said with a shy grin.

Sam shook his head. "Look, I really must ask you to leave. It's getting late, and I'm tired. So, why don't you run along now so I can finish my work and go to bed?"

"OK," Jackie responded with a smile. "I left my bike by the highway. I'll just go now." She moved to a small door beside the large hangar entrance. "Just one question."

"What?"

"Which way is the highway? I kinda lost my bearings when you almost landed on me."

Sam closed his eyes and sighed. Then he walked briskly over and grabbed a flashlight from a recharging unit on the wall by the hanger door. He switched the flashlight on, sending a bright beam through the quiet confines of the spacious hangar. Swinging open the smaller door, he motioned for his visitor to follow. "Come on, I'll show you where it is."

Following the glowing pool created by Sam's flashlight, the two walked without speaking across the dark field. Jackie glanced up at her companion. "What do you do when you're scared?" she asked.

Sam lifted his chin. "I don't get scared very often."

Jackie nodded. "I wish I were you, because I get scared a lot."

"Of what?"

"Oh, spiders, really big dogs, school, and . . . going to my aunt's house."

Sam stopped walking. "You're not saying that—"

"Oh, no, my aunt doesn't do anything bad to me. She just doesn't do *anything*. And she doesn't want me to be there. It's kinda scary living in a place where you're not wanted—do you know what I mean?"

Sam resumed his pace. "Actually, I do. Sometimes the world isn't a nice place."

"So, what do you do when you get scared?"

"I fly."

"Really?"

Sam pointed. "OK, here we are by the road. Where did you leave your bike?"

Jackie glanced around. "There it is. Over there." She ran to where the bicycle lay half-hidden in the tall grasses edging the highway. "I really appreciate your help. I guess you're not so mean after all." Picking up her bicycle, she swung it around to face the lights of the little town that glowed a mile or so to the west. "Guess I'll be going now. Can't exactly get lost in Wisconsin. See?" She pointed down the road. "No curves."

With a wave, she pedaled away, her retreating form quickly swallowed whole by the darkness. "I'll come see you again if you promise not to chop me up with an Aztec," Sam heard her call over her shoulder.

"That won't be necessary," he responded into the darkness. "Really."

There was no answer, just the hoot of a distant

owl and the soft rustle of dry leaves shifting in the gentle breeze. With a shake of his head, Sam turned and made his way back toward the hangar waiting at the far side of the broad, flat field.

\* \* \* \* \*

Jackie squirmed in her seat as she glanced at the wall clock hanging above Miss Leyland's desk. Ten-thirty. She'd been at school for only two-and-a-half hours, and already it seemed like the day should be over. Funny thing was, back in Cyprus Hill she'd loved going to school. She'd been surrounded by friends like Alex Timmons, Alicia and Shane Curtain, and a whole Pathfinder Club full of young people who made her life interesting. Here, the only person besides Miss Leyland who paid her any attention at all was a girl named Brenda. That girl had short-cropped brown hair and dark eyes, and she sat two rows up and one row over from Jackie's desk. Jackie decided that, if given a choice, she'd rather face last night's flying food grinder than deal with the likes of Brenda.

Jackie reached into her desk and took out a small, orange-and-black badge from her pencil box. It sported an image of a cooking pot with a long handle and represented a Pathfinder honor that she and other club members had earned just before she left Cyprus Hill—before her life changed from good to horrible.

"Miss Leyland," Jackie heard Brenda call in her high-pitched, totally annoying voice.

"Yes, Brenda," the neatly dressed woman at the whiteboard responded without turning from her writing.

"Jackie isn't studying," Brenda announced loud enough for the entire class to hear. "She's just staring at something she got out of her desk. Now, Miss Leyland, I know that you've worked very hard to prepare today's math lesson, and we, your students, should show our respect by paying attention to your every word. So it just breaks my heart to see someone like Jackie Anderson blatantly ignoring your capable and, may I say, very professional instructions. With your permission, I'll be happy to report her to Principal Hart."

Miss Leyland stopped writing and closed her eyes. With a sigh, she turned to face the room. "Brenda," she said, "why don't you just concentrate on your own work instead of worrying about what Jackie is doing, OK?"

"Excellent idea," Brenda responded with a sugary smile, "although it's hard for me to concentrate when a classmate like Jackie insists on being disruptive by not paying attention to you, our teacher. But I'll do my best. I guess that in West Virginia, students aren't as refined as we are here in Wisconsin. Besides, we shouldn't expect much from a hillbilly."

"At least we've got hills," Jackie shot back.

"We've got them, too," Brenda retorted. "Ours are just more . . . refined."

"You mean flat!"

"Girls, girls!" Miss Leyland called, hurrying up the aisle. "I won't have you disrupting our class with your petty arguing. If you don't quiet down, I'll report you *both* to Principal Hart."

"Well, she started it," Brenda whined. "I was just minding my own business when she began bothering me."

"I opened my desk!" Jackie shot back. "Students do that all the time."

"Not when I'm trying to figure out 156 divided by 12 plus 17."

"Thirty," Jackie announced without missing a beat.

Miss Leyland paused, thought for a moment, and then her eyes opened wide. "Why, that's correct, Jackie."

Jackie smiled shyly. "I . . . I'm pretty good at math. Top of my class in Cyprus Hill."

Brenda stood and faced her classmate. "Yeah, and you probably learned your numbers counting the money your mother stole."

Jackie jumped to her feet. "You take that back. You take that back this instant!"

"Whoa, whoa, *whoa!*" Miss Leyland demanded, trying to be heard above the verbal attacks being hurled up and down the row of desks. "If you two don't stop, I'll send you both to detention. Do you hear me?"

Jackie stopped speaking mid-sentence. "Yes, ma'am," she responded quietly, returning to her seat.

Brenda stood red-faced, almost vibrating with anger. "Yes, Miss Leyland," she agreed reluctantly. Then she whirled around and sat down with an angry sigh, her arms tightly folded in front of her.

Jackie felt like bursting into tears. This wasn't the way she acted in school. In the past, she'd never caused a teacher one moment of grief. Threats of detention had never been part of her educational experience. Now, it seemed, she spent large portions of her days at this new school either embarrassed or angry—two emotions that were becoming far too familiar.

She returned the cooking honor patch to its place in her pencil box, closed the top of her desk, and tried to concentrate on her studies. Glancing up, she noticed Brenda staring at her. She knew she hadn't heard the last from this unpleasant classmate.

Jackie closed her eyes and thought of Cyprus Hill, imagining the trees and mountains surrounding the quiet town; the shouts of playmates echoing from Benson Park; the friendly looks on the faces of her friends. She remembered her mother's loving smile and her father's boisterous laughter, the kind that filled the house and spilled like a bubbling stream out onto the lawn and beyond. Why had they been so stupid? Why had they made such horrible choices—such destructive errors in judgment that had cost them all their happiness?

A single tear trickled down Jackie's face as memories carried her away from Wisconsin, to a time and place where joy had been a constant companion.

# Chapter 2

# Lentil Soup

"Is that you?" a voice called from the kitchen as Jackie entered the small, two-story home on McCoy Street.

"Yes, Aunt Elsa," Jackie answered while lowering her backpack and removing her shoes.

"Remember to take off your shoes."

"Yes, Aunt Elsa," Jackie said. "Shoes are off."

"And mind your backpack. I don't want it scratching my coffee table."

Jackie grabbed her pack and quickly lifted it off the coffee table just as her aunt entered the living room. The stocky, middle-aged woman sported a head of short-cropped blond hair and a dress that was a couple sizes too small. She wobbled across the room on high-heeled shoes that Jackie figured must feel even more uncomfortable than they looked. A lighted cigarette dangled from her mouth and bobbed up and down as she spoke, sending little showers of ash onto her chest.

"One thing I can't stand is a messy floor . . . and scratches," she said, hurrying over to the closet, where she took her purse and car keys down from a shelf. "I bought you a can of soup for supper. Just open and pour it into a pan, or pot, or whatever you use to cook things. I've got a date, so don't expect me back anytime soon. And try not to clutter the house. I don't like clutter either. Did you have a good day at school?"

Jackie opened her mouth to respond, but before she could say anything, her aunt said, "Good. That's great. Now, gotta go." Then, with a half-hearted wave, she hurried through the front door amid a blue haze of cigarette smoke and drifting ash. Jackie heard her heels clicking down the sidewalk, followed by the sound of a car engine roaring to life and heading down the street, and then all was quiet.

"No, I didn't have a good day at school," Jackie said to no one. "As a matter of fact, I had a lousy day. Would you like to hear about it?" She paused as if waiting for an answer. "Very well then, I'll tell you. Brenda was her usual royal pain, I got kicked twice during soccer, Miss Leyland threatened to send me to detention, and a dog almost bit me on the elbow while I was coming back from the bus stop. Someone put salt in my lemonade during lunch, I got called a 'hillbilly' four times, and I think I may have accidentally put my history book in the wrong locker. Other than that, everything was just peachy."

Jackie walked into the kitchen, where she noticed the promised can of soup sitting alone on the shiny island. Opening the refrigerator door, she stood staring at mostly barren shelves. Even the freezer section was vacant except for a half-empty carton of chocolate ice cream that had been there when she'd moved in more than a month ago.

"What shall I fix for supper?" she asked herself aloud, examining the barren cupboards and unused pantry. "Pizza? Spaghetti with angel hair pasta and marinara sauce? Sleepy-time stew?" Picking up the can, she added, "Or, how about a nice, steaming bowl of lentil soup topped off with a refreshing serving of month-old chocolate ice cream? Why, that sounds delicious. Or, I can do like my Aunt Elsa does and simply go out to a restaurant every day with some loser, and then eat the leftovers for breakfast. Quick, easy, cheap. Don't need a food budget when you can bum your living off of someone else."

Jackie sighed. "I know, I know," she chastised herself. "I shouldn't say bad things about Aunt Elsa." Then she giggled. "Who am I kidding? Let's just say she's an opportunist, someone who gets by on her natural wit and endless charm."

Jackie picked up the container of soup and studied it thoughtfully. Suddenly, she smiled. Running into the living room, she grabbed her backpack, emptied its contents on the couch, dropped the can into the dark recesses of her book bag, and hurried out the door.

* * * * *

Sam Fieldstone adjusted the propeller pitch control of the Cessna 182 he was flying and set the mixture at full rich. Smoothly, he reduced the throttle and lowered the nose slightly, setting up a shallow glide toward the distant grass runway neatly carved out of the trees filling his fifty-acre property. He lowered the wing flaps and fingered the trim knob until the aircraft held its angle even without his hands on the yolk. The air was silky smooth, just the way he liked it. In these conditions, it felt like the Cessna was hovering and the ground was rotating slowly beneath him.

He smiled. The roughness of the engine had vanished, thanks to a good cleaning of the spark plugs and a much-needed replacement of the fuel filters. He'd made some other adjustments here and there using techniques he'd learned during years of working in and around such aircraft. The owner would be pleased.

With a soft whistle of air and the rattle of rubber and metal, the plane settled onto the surface of the field and rolled along, content to be back to earth after its shakedown flight at the hands of the experienced pilot/mechanic who'd skillfully returned it to perfect working order.

Sam revved the engine and guided the aircraft toward the hangar just as the sun was touching the western horizon. When the propeller stopped spinning, he toggled off the electrical switches and exited the cockpit, eager to sign off another job in the airplane's maintenance logs.

As he was entering his name and mechanic's license number on the appropriate page, he stopped and sniffed the air. Frowning, he looked around the hangar. Then he walked to the door leading into the small kitchen he'd built for himself in the back of the barn's roomy expanse. There he found a table set attractively with a colorful cloth, two bowls, two glasses, and carefully positioned silverware lying atop folded paper napkins. At the gas stove stood Jackie Anderson, a big smile lighting her face. "You like lentil soup?" she asked cheerfully.

"Ah . . . sure," Sam said. "What are you doing here again?"

"Fixing supper," came the quick reply. "What does it look like I'm doing? My dad always said, 'A man's gotta eat.' Well, you're a man, and this is lentil soup. I bought some whole wheat bread at the store on the way over so we can have sandwiches. Hope you like tomato and lettuce. My favorite. Healthy, too."

"You shouldn't be doing this," Sam said, eyeing the steaming pot bubbling on the stove.

"Well," Jackie responded with a shy grin. "I figured I owed you, seeing as how I messed up your landing last night."

"I landed just fine in spite of you."

"Oh, I'm sure you did. I also felt bad about making you walk me all the way back to the road in the dark. By the way, after supper, would you mind walking me back to the road again? That's where I left my bicycle."

"Why didn't you ride down my driveway?"

"Oh, I couldn't do that."

"Why?"

"That would be trespassing."

Sam grinned before he could stop himself. Turning, he walked back through the hangar to complete his logbook entries. "Just don't make a habit of coming here and bothering me," he called over his shoulder.

"Did you know that the milk in your refrigerator is out of date?" he heard Jackie say. "The missing child on the carton has been found and has kids of her own now."

"You're very funny," Sam called back. Then he paused. "Hey, kid?"

"Yeah?"

"How'd your aunt treat you today?"

"About the same. She did buy me a can of lentil soup."

"Does she know you're here?"

Jackie appeared at the kitchen door, empty serving bowl in her hands. "No."

"I just don't want her to think I kidnapped you or something."

Jackie laughed. "If someone did, she wouldn't notice."

"That's no way to treat a child," Sam said.

"Hey, I'm not a child. I'm almost thirteen! Why, in just over three years, I'll be old enough to solo in one of your silly airplanes."

Sam blinked. "How'd you know that?"

"Looked it up on the Internet at school. You

can solo at sixteen. Fly all by yourself—under an instructor's supervision, of course."

Sam nodded as he continued to write in the aircraft engine log. "You're pretty smart for a trespasser."

Jackie returned to her work at the stove. "So, Mr. Fieldstone, what did *you* do today? Land on anybody I know?"

Sam closed the logs and slipped them into the glove compartment of the Cessna. "As long as you insist on fixing me supper, I guess you can call me Sam."

"OK. And you can call me Jackie. I like that better than *kid* or *child* or *hey you*."

"Fine. And to answer your question: No, you're the only person I've tried to land on lately." Sam glanced at his watch. "Are you almost done? I've got someone stopping by soon."

"Hot date?"

"No, customer. Belongs to this Cessna Skylane."

Jackie appeared again at the kitchen door. "In that case, supper is served. Go wash your hands."

"I don't have to wash my hands in my own house."

"I thought you said this was a hangar."

Sam strolled into the kitchen and sat down on one of the chairs standing beside the attractively set table. "It also happens to be my home. I've got a cot over on the far wall."

"You sleep in a barn?"

"*Hangar!* It's a *hangar!* And yes, I sleep here. I just happen to like airplanes. They're good company—they don't make demands; they don't ask a bunch of stupid questions every time I see them; and they don't just show up unannounced, like some people I know."

"Well," Jackie countered, "can an airplane fix you a delicious, healthy supper of lentil soup and lettuce and tomato sandwiches?"

Sam shook his head and smiled slightly. "Actually, no. It can't."

"So, there you are. You need me."

Before Sam could answer, Jackie took his stained and greasy hand in hers and bowed her head. "Hey, God," she said quietly. "It's me again." Self-consciously, Sam bowed his head as well, keeping his gaze fixed on Jackie. "I know we haven't spoken for a while," she continued, "but tonight is special. This is Sam Fieldstone. He probably wouldn't mind it if You called him Sam. He's a pilot. You may have seen him flying around up there in Your sky. Anyway, we want to thank You for this food and for this nice barn that is really a hangar. Please keep Sam safe as he fixes and flies airplanes, because he really likes doing that. Amen."

Sam sat staring at Jackie for a long moment. No one had ever mentioned his name in prayer before. No one had ever talked to God about his work and his passion for flying. In all the years that he'd moved among the clouds, he'd never ceased to wonder at the power of nature on display far below, at the endless movement of weather systems and the mysterious forces keeping his aircraft aloft. He'd often wondered if there was a God holding everything together, but he'd never taken the time to find out. It was enough for him to wonder. It was enough for him to fly.

But, now, listening to Jackie speak to her God in such an innocent way, hearing her introduce him to that puzzling power, stirred something deep inside him. It was a longing to know more, to understand, to find answers to the many questions that chased him through the sky.

Jackie, her mouth full of sandwich, glanced over at her companion and frowned. "Eat," she said, speaking the word between chews. "Then maybe you won't be so grouchy."

Sam nodded and picked up his sandwich. "Thank you," he said before taking his first bite.

"You're welcome," Jackie responded. "I might not be an airplane, but I'm a pretty good cook."

With that, she attacked her supper with even more determination. The two ate in silence, each enjoying the serenity that comes from not being alone.

# Chapter 3

# Sturgeon Bay

Jackie had just finished washing the supper dishes in the small kitchen when she heard Sam call her name. Stepping out into the hangar, she noticed that the old pilot was standing near the nose of the Cessna, and a very distinguished-looking woman stood beside him. The visitor wore a blue jumpsuit, and she had pulled her soft brown hair into a ponytail. But it was her face that held Jackie's gaze. The woman's smile was wide and genuine, her blue eyes kind and inviting.

"Jackie, get over here," Sam ordered with a wave. "I want you to meet someone. I was just telling her about you. This is Dr. Christina Taylor. She's from Oshkosh."

Jackie frowned. "Is someone sick?"

The woman extended a perfectly manicured hand toward Jackie. "I'm a dentist," she said.

"Oh," Jackie responded, "does someone have sick teeth?"

Sam and his visitor laughed. "I hope not," the woman said. "I'm just here to pick up my airplane."

"*Your* airplane?" Jackie gasped. "You're a pilot?"

Sam motioned first at the Cessna, then at the woman. "This beauty belongs to that beauty," he said, causing his visitor to blush shyly.

Jackie grinned. "Wow! A woman pilot. Did Sam teach you how to fly?"

"No," the woman said. "I used to live in Chicago. I had a dental practice downtown near the El. After I learned to fly, I kept my Skylane out at an airport called Meigs Field. When the mayor closed Meigs Field, my plane and I packed our bags and flew north to Oshkosh. I was getting kind of tired of the big city anyway.

"After I found an airport with available hangar space, I asked around for the name of a good mechanic. One kept popping up: Sam Fieldstone. So, ever since, Sam has been keeping my air chariot up and running." The woman patted the nose of her aircraft lovingly. "But, sadly, I may be in the market for a simpler aircraft. I don't make many long trips anymore." She paused, and then smiled at Jackie. "Do you like flying?"

The girl thought for a moment. "Probably."

"You've never been up?"

"Nope. But Sam almost landed on me last night, if that counts."

The woman turned to face the mechanic. "You did what?"

"Don't listen to her," Sam said. Then, attempting to change the subject quickly, he pointed at the Skylane. "So, I've got your bird all ready to go.

Shouldn't give you any more roughness problems. You can fly her back to Wittman tonight if you want."

Dr. Taylor's grin widened. "That's great, Sam," she said with genuine affection. "You're the best. And thanks for letting me use your car for the last couple days." Turning back to the girl, she added, "Jackie, why don't I take you for a ride sometime. Would you like that?"

"Sure. When?"

"How about Sunday? We can head north. Maybe even fly up to Green Bay. Might see some wildlife along the way."

"Sounds great!"

"Of course, you should check with your aunt first."

Jackie chuckled. "Tell you what, if I see her between now and then, I'll ask."

Dr. Taylor studied the young girl for a moment. "Sam told me about your parents. Tough break."

Jackie shrugged, but said nothing.

"So, I'll see you bright and early on Sunday, OK?"

"OK."

With that, the woman handed a check to the mechanic, and the two pushed the aircraft around until it pointed in the direction of the open field. Jackie watched as the pretty pilot climbed aboard, fastened herself in, and closed the door. Then, following a printed checklist she held in her hand, she began checking the instruments and switches one by one. When she was through, she swung open the small side window and shouted, "Clear!" The black propeller turned round and round and round until the engine roared to life. Before long, the dentist and her precious Skylane were racing down the grass strip. Smoothly, effortlessly, they climbed into the star-littered sky, the aircraft's position and recognition lights glowing and blinking brightly in the inky darkness.

"How cool is that?" Jackie murmured, watching as the airplane became just another light in the vast, sparkling canopy overhead.

"Tell me about it," Sam responded with a satisfied grin.

The two walked back into the hangar, where Sam retrieved his trusty flashlight from the hook by the door. "You ready to go?" he asked.

"Yup," Jackie said. Then she paused. "Just let me get my jacket." Sam watched as she scurried around the two airplanes parked in the hangar and headed for the kitchen. When she came back into sight, she was pushing her arms into her thin blue coat. Suddenly, she stopped. "Hey, Sam," she called, changing direction and heading for a door half hidden behind a battered golf cart and an old, rusted motorcycle frame. "What's in—?"

"Stay away from there!" the mechanic shouted, his voice suddenly stern, almost angry.

Jackie, shocked by Sam's sudden outburst, stepped back quickly. "Why?" she asked.

Sam cleared his throat. "I . . . I just don't want people rummaging around in my hangar, that's all. Leave that room alone, do you hear me?"

Jackie glanced at the door and then back at the man. "Sure," she said as an uncomfortable fear tickled her stomach. "I'll . . . I won't snoop around so much, I promise. I don't want to wear out my welcome, you know." She walked up to the pilot, attempting a smile. "I . . . I haven't worn out my welcome, have I?"

Wordlessly, Sam motioned for her to follow, and the two headed out across the dark field, led by the bright, white pool created by Sam's flashlight. The evening air was cold and slightly damp, and a breeze ruffled the grasses and weeds lining the landing strip.

When they reached the side of the road, Sam pointed in the direction of the bike. "There's your ride," he said. Then he hesitated, as if searching for the right words to say. "Listen, Jackie. You really shouldn't leave your bike out beside the highway like this. It's not safe, . . . and, well, it would be better if you didn't do it."

Jackie nodded as a deep sadness rose in her chest, making it hard for her to breath. Now she'd done it. She'd made him really angry. Whatever was behind that door, whatever was in that room at the back of the hangar, had destroyed whatever relationship she thought she was developing with the strange man who lived in a barn.

"I think . . ." Sam continued hesitatingly, "I think that you—"

"What?" Jackie asked, afraid of what he was about to say.

"I think . . . that you . . . should use the driveway next time."

Jackie blinked. "Did you say 'next time'?"

"That is, if you want to stop by or something. Besides, you'll be coming out on Sunday, right?"

"Right."

"So, you should use the driveway. It starts right down there by those trees." The mechanic paused. "And another thing, Jackie, you really shouldn't be riding your bicycle out here on the highway without some kind of light on it. While it's not a busy road, sometimes people do whiz by here kinda fast. So, I'll see if I can find you a light that you can use so that . . . you know . . . they can see you . . . at night . . . here."

With a happy cry, Jackie threw her arms around the man, giving him a quick hug. Then she hopped onto her bicycle. "I hope you like spaghetti," she called over her shoulder as she pedaled away.

"You don't have to feed me," Sam said. "I know how to buy food!"

"Like you know how to buy milk?" Jackie responded, her voice echoing back over the expanding distance behind them.

"Spaghetti would be fine," Sam shouted. "But you don't have to . . . I mean . . ."

But Jackie was gone, and all Sam heard was the hoot of the owl somewhere deep in the nearby woods. With a shake of his head and a soft chuckle, he started back across the field in the direction of the hangar. Halfway there, he stopped and looked up at the night sky, wondering if it was true. Was there, in fact, a God who watched over him, who was interested in his life, his work, and his flying? Could he really speak to Him just by bowing his head and talking? Suddenly, he felt his fingers curl to form tight fists at his side. If there was such a God, where was He that night when—?

Sam closed his eyes as if to shut out a horrible sight. Then, with a sigh, he continued on his way, heading for the warmth and security of his hangar home. Some questions, it seemed, were too painful to ask, even when talking to someone else's God.

\* \* \* \* \*

"You can open your eyes now."

Jackie shook her head.

"Really. It's OK. We're safely up in the air. Everything's fine. The view's fantastic. I think you'll like it."

Dr. Taylor's shiny Cessna glided over the flat countryside, cruising effortlessly at 145 miles per hour, moving through the cool, autumn air fifty-five hundred feet above the ground. The pilot grinned as she watched her passenger's fingers begin to part, allowing the eyes hidden behind to see the lofty world of the private pilot for the first time.

Jackie peeked one way and then another, catching quick glances of the sunlit cockpit and the vast spread of land far below. She noticed a large body of water off to their left.

"Lake Winnebago," the pilot announced, watching Jackie's fingers part a little more. "That's Oshkosh on the far side. See the airport south of town? And if you'll look to the east, that way, you'll see Lake Michigan in the distance."

Gazing out past the right wing of the aircraft, Jackie could see the smooth, shimmering surface of the huge, freshwater lake lining the horizon. "Wow!" she breathed quietly. "Wow."

"Now, Jackie," the pilot said, "I'm going to bank the airplane a little to the right, OK? The wings will tilt so that we can fly in a new direction. You ready?"

Jackie nodded, grabbing the armrest built into the door beside her. The Skylane tilted slightly, and the world rotated slowly far below. Then everything returned to the way it was before, except now all the views had changed. "That's called 'turning to a new heading' in airplane talk. It wasn't so bad, was it?"

The girl shook her head.

"I thought we'd head up to Sturgeon Bay," the pretty pilot continued, "to a beautiful place right near the water. I brought along a picnic lunch. We can eat in Bay View Park and then visit the Maritime Museum. How about it? Are you with me?"

Jackie kept her grip on the armrest. "We're a thousand miles up in the air, and you're the only one who knows how to fly this thing. How can I not be with you?"

Dr. Taylor laughed. "Good point. But I'll take good care of you, don't worry. We'll have a great time together, OK?"

Jackie relaxed just a little, still a bit unsure of herself. "Dr. Taylor," she said after studying the distant horizon for a long moment, "why are you doing this?"

"Call me Tina," the pilot responded with a smile. " 'Dr. Taylor' sounds so formal, as if you've come to have your teeth pulled."

"OK . . . Tina. Why are you doing this?"

"Doing what?"

"Treating me so nicely. Taking me for a ride in your really scary airplane. Spending the day trying to make me happy. You don't even know me."

The woman gazed out through the windshield. "Actually, I do know you," she said. "At least, I sort of understand what you're going through. You see, my husband left me a few years back. He fell in love with another woman. He and I had been in business together, operating a dental clinic in Chicago. After the divorce was finalized, I had a hard time adjusting to being on my own again, and, well, I determined that if I ever met someone who was lonely, I'd try to do something about it—you know, help a little. From what Sam has told me, you sound like you might be a little lonely. Just moved to a new town, haven't had time to develop any friendships, live with an aunt who doesn't pay much attention to you. That must be a bit . . . confusing."

Jackie shrugged. "My parents got what they deserved. They're crooks." She studied the farmland slipping by below. "Not even God could help them."

Tina nodded slowly. She recognized the hurt, the defensive words, and the denial that often accompanies the pain of separation. She'd experienced those same emotions in her own life, and her heart ached for her passenger. "We'll be there in about twenty minutes," she announced, trying to sound cheery. "You'll see a little town nestled beside a lovely harbor. The airport will be due west. It has two runways that cross in the middle. A cab should be waiting for us when we land." She glanced over at her passenger. "Are you hungry?"

She saw Jackie's head bob up and down. "Good. Me too," Tina said. "I could eat a goat."

Jackie turned. "I'm a vegetarian," she announced.

"Me too!" Tina responded. "I meant to say, 'I could eat a soy goat.'"

Jackie giggled and then burst out laughing. "With grass milk and bark bread?" she asked.

"Yup," Tina said. "And all covered with leaf gravy."

The two stared at each other for a moment and then both shouted, *"Yuuuck!"*

Tina's Cessna continued its journey through the morning air, heading northeast, following the finger of land that stretched from the city of Green Bay to Washington Island. Forested fields and open pastureland created a rich mosaic of color and texture below, their patchwork framed on two sides by the deep blue waters of Lake Michigan.

Before long, Tina reduced the engine's power and lowered the nose of her aircraft to begin a long, shallow glide toward a distant airport. Jackie could see the quaint town of Sturgeon Bay off to the right, nestled by a peaceful inlet stretching west to east. Low bridges spanned the sparkling waters fronting the picturesque community.

After landing, Tina taxied the Skylane to the little general aviation office at the south end of the airport. While they were tying the airplane down, the taxicab arrived. Soon the two adventurers found themselves riding a little lower to the ground as the car carried them across one of the bridges Jackie had seen from the air.

Bay View Park lived up to its name perfectly. It provided an unrestricted view of the waters of Sturgeon Bay as well as peeks at several shipbuilding facilities and an endless variety of boats moving along the waterway. The two selected a picnic table under the branches of a tree, and Tina unloaded the contents of the large shopping bag she'd carried from home. In minutes, they were enjoying thick peanut-butter-and-jelly sandwiches, crunchy corn chips, and crisp baby carrots. They washed everything down with soymilk served in little cartons. Jackie insisted that they were really drinking goat's milk.

"So," she said between bites of carrots and slurps of milk, "your husband left you for another woman, huh? Was she pretty?"

Tina nodded. "Totally. She looked like a model in one of those fashion magazines. Tall. Blond hair—*real* blond hair. Gorgeous eyes. The works."

"Well, you're pretty, too," Jackie said.

"That's nice of you to say," Tina responded with an appreciative smile.

"My mom is pretty," Jackie said. "Not like in a fashion magazine. More like in a sweet, friendly, best-friend kind of way. Know what I mean?"

"Tell me about her," Tina invited.

Jackie thought for a minute. "She always wanted the best. You know—prettiest dresses, biggest TV, fanciest car. Let's just say she liked to show off to the neighbors. That's probably why she stole the money from the insurance company, so she could buy stuff that we couldn't afford."

"And your dad?"

"He had this drug problem. I mean, he wasn't like a junkie lying in a gutter or anything, and he didn't go around selling it. He had a really cool job at a local sand mine, driving a *huge* dump truck. He worked hard, and once in a while he'd even go to church with me. But I guess he got hooked on crack one day. We wouldn't have known anything about it except one night Sheriff Curtain, the head cop in Cyprus Hill, tried to stop my dad to tell him that the taillights on his car weren't working. Well, Dad freaked out because he had this little bag of white powder in the car with him. He put the pedal to the metal and tried to outrun the flashing light in his rearview mirror. Really dumb idea. When the sheriff caught him, he found the drugs and tossed dad in jail. End of story."

Tina studied Jackie thoughtfully. "How'd all that make you feel?"

Jackie watched a fishing boat bob past the park, leaving a widening wake behind it in the deep blue of the water. "Kinda worthless," she said quietly. "I mean, both my parents chose to do things that are illegal. They must have known that if they were caught, they'd lose everything, including me." Tina noticed the deep sadness reflected in Jackie's eyes as she turned to face her. "Aren't I more important than a new TV or a stupid drug fix?" she asked. "Aren't I worth anything at all?"

"I think you are," Tina said softly.

"Well, you're the only one who does," Jackie said. "Not even God cares. I prayed myself silly when all of this was happening. Read the Bible, sang songs, doubled my offerings at church. But nothing happened. Nothing at all."

"Sounds like your parents—"

"Sam is one truly weird person, don't you think?"

Tina blinked at the sudden change of subject. "Ah . . . absolutely," she said.

"And let me tell you," Jackie said, lifting a warning finger, "whatever you do, don't go near that room in the back of the hangar, the one behind the golf cart. He'll eat you alive."

Tina nodded slowly. "We all have secrets we need to hide," she said.

Jackie's eyes opened wide. "Do you know what's in that room?"

The woman began gathering up the crumpled sandwich wraps, used napkins, and empty milk cartons, tossing them into the shopping bag. "I've heard stories," she said. "People talk. But it's really none of my business, so I don't ask any questions."

Jackie glanced out across the bay and sighed a contented sigh. "This is nice," she said. "I'm really glad you brought me here."

"Well, I'm glad you like it," Tina declared, rising to her feet and stretching in the bright sunlight filtering down through the branches. "But we're not done yet. We've got to go visit the Door County Maritime Museum and Lighthouse Preservation Society."

"Wow," Jackie gasped as she, too, stood to her feet. "That's a big name for a museum. What are we going to see?"

"Let's go find out."

The two hurried away, moving happily among the tourists strolling about the park.

\* \* \* \* \*

"How was it?" Sam shouted as Jackie stepped down from the airplane and stood behind the open passenger-side door of Tina's Cessna.

"Outstanding!" Jackie said, trying to be heard over the rush of air and the drone of the idling engine. "I even got to fly the airplane on the way back. First I zoomed this way," she said, tilting her hand toward her right, "then I zoomed this way." Her hand moved majestically to the left. "I love flying. I mean I *love* flying. I'm going to be a pilot in three years, and you can teach me. I think I'm pretty good at it already because we didn't crash or hit any small children or anything."

"Slow down there, girl," Sam urged as he winked at Tina, who remained in her seat in the airplane, readying the Cessna for a quick turnaround and departure. "Let's let Dr. Taylor leave. She needs to get back to Oshkosh before the weather changes."

Jackie turned and gave a thumbs-up to her smiling friend. Then she helped Sam latch the door closed. The two moved away from the aircraft as it taxied toward the open field, blasting them with a rush of cold wind.

Tina waved as the aircraft raced down the grass strip and rose smoothly into the air. Jackie saw her rock the wings back and forth before she banked toward the lake the girl now knew lay to the west. A line of dark clouds marched across the distant horizon, blocking the sun, announcing that the run of good autumn weather that they'd been enjoying for the past couple weeks was about to end.

"You'd better head home, too," Sam said as he and Jackie walked into the hangar. "Don't want to you to be caught out in the storm either."

The girl nodded. "OK. But I just have to tell you what an awesome day we had. The flight was totally cool, and we had a picnic in a little park where you can see the boats going by and people catching really ugly fish, and we visited a museum that showed stuff about shipbuilding, lighthouses, and even had a periscope to look through. Oh, and there was a pilothouse from an actual freighter. Did you know that boats have pilots, too? I didn't know that until today. It was really, really neat. And Tina is so much fun. We had a great time."

"I'm sure you did," Sam said with a smile, "but now you've got to hit the road, young lady. I want you back in town before it gets dark. And that's an order."

"Yes sir, Captain Fieldstone."

"Don't call me that!" the man said abruptly. Then he softened a little. "I . . . I just don't want you to catch cold, OK?"

"Sure," Jackie said, wondering why her companion had snapped at her again. "I'll pedal as fast as I can, OK?"

"OK," Sam responded.

As Jackie approached her bicycle leaning against the hangar wall, she stopped and stared. "Hey, look," she called. "Someone put a great big light on my bike. Now, I wonder who did that." She admired the shiny, streamlined device fastened securely to the handlebars. "Perhaps it was the bike fairy. Did you see a bike fairy here today, Sam?"

The man chuckled. "Get out of here," he ordered with a grin. "And don't go shining that thing all over the place. Just use it when you need to see where you're going. It runs on batteries, and they don't last forever. Now *get!*"

Jackie threw her leg over the curving center bar. "Thanks, Sam," she said as she guided her two-wheeler out into the evening air. "You're the best."

The man shrugged. "I just want to help you get home," he called. As he watched her pedal down the long driveway leading to the highway, he added softly, ". . . wherever that is."

Reentering the hangar, he pressed a switch on the wall, causing the big door to swing slowly into position and shut him away from the approaching weather. Walking toward the kitchen, he paused and stared at the door behind the battered golf cart. He remained motionless, standing in the soft light for a long moment, a look of sadness shadowing his tired face. Then he moved on, motivated by the hot cup of tea he'd promised to prepare for himself at the end of his day.

# Chapter 4

# A Mysterious Gift

Jackie sat watching raindrops strike her bedroom window with muffled plops. Outside, the cold air was heavy with moisture. The street lamp that hung over the cracked sidewalk in front of the house did little to chase the darkness away.

She sighed, glancing down at her schoolbooks and the assorted homework papers that she'd filled with carefully written letters and neat rows of numbers. Math, history, geography—all done. She'd even read a chapter ahead in her English book. *It's amazing how much stuff you can do when you don't have a life,* she thought to herself.

The weather had even forced her to keep her bicycle tucked away in the safety of the little garage by the house. She hadn't wanted to face the storms and the heavy rains that had soaked central Wisconsin for the past four days.

Jackie had thought about calling Sam, except that the only phone in the house stayed hidden in her aunt's well-guarded purse. She had asked to use it a couple times. But that had set Aunt

Elsa off. She had complained about how expensive cell phone calls were. And she had said that twelve-year-old girls shouldn't get in the habit of talking to anyone and everyone just because they felt like it. Of course, this hadn't kept Aunt Elsa from chatting on her cell phone for hours.

Even the amount of mail Jackie had received since moving to Lakeside had dwindled from a trickle to an all-out drought. She understood. Her classmates and the kids she knew from church back in Cyprus Hill had more interesting things to do than write to a lonely girl in faraway Wisconsin.

Jackie smiled when she thought about her old Pathfinder club, especially that one particular Pathfinder named Alex Timmons, a boy with enough energy to power a small city. "I wonder what trouble he and the members of his Honors Club are getting into?" she asked aloud, chuckling softly to herself.

She pulled open the drawer of her desk and picked up a tattered book, one that listed every Pathfinder honor available. She opened it and then quickly closed it again, tossing it back among the pencils, markers, and other homework-related essentials. Why tease herself with what used to be? Why bother dreaming impossible dreams? Lakeside had no Pathfinder club. It didn't even have a church like the one she had left. Life was different now. She'd just have to learn to live with that fact.

A knock sounded at her bedroom door. "Hey Jackie, you in there?" She recognized the slightly slurred voice of her aunt.

"Yes."

"Well, I got something for you. Open up."

Jackie sighed and walked across the room. Opening the door, she stood facing her Aunt Elsa. The way the woman acted and looked provided convincing clues to her condition. The bitter smell of alcohol flowed into the room, along with a strong scent of roses. The more tolerable of the two odors came from the perfume in which Aunt Elsa doused herself daily. "This came today," the woman announced. She held out a long, narrow package with Jackie's name printed neatly on the label. "Now listen, young lady," she continued, obviously annoyed, "I can't have all this mail coming to this address day after day. I mean I've got better things to do than play UPS for you."

Jackie chuckled. "Aunt Elsa, this is the only package I've received since I arrived over a month ago."

The woman frowned. "That's one package too many. I'm not your delivery man, so cut it out."

"Yes, ma'am," Jackie said with a nod. "You can leave any other packages that arrive for me right there on the front porch. I will personally carry them into the house and across the front room to this door. You won't have to lift a finger. Deal?"

Aunt Elsa thought for a moment, trying to grasp the image of Jackie carrying her own mail from the porch to the little guest room. Eventually, she said, "Deal," still not fully understanding what she was agreeing to. Then she turned and shuffled away, mumbling under her breath that her life was not her own since this *child* had been forced upon her against her will.

Jackie closed the door and stood looking down at the mysterious parcel. The return address was somewhere in Massachusetts.

Massachusetts? Whom did she know there? No one.

Jackie sat down at her desk. Resting the package atop her piles of papers and books, she examined it carefully. *Well,* she said to herself, *there's only one way to find out what's inside.*

Grabbing her letter opener, she slit the shipping tape covering the end of the parcel and slowly opened the flap. Inside, she found another box that was the same shape as the first, only slightly smaller. As she pulled it out, a gasp of wonder and delight escaped her lips. In her hands, she held a long blue box with a blue-and-yellow airplane pictured on the cover. Two men wearing baseball caps sat, one in front of the other, inside the craft. Printed in black letters were the words "Piper Super Cub 95." On the far right of the box she read, "Authentic Flying Scale Model Airplane, balsawood construction kit."

"An airplane!" Jackie breathed, hardly able to contain her excitement. "Someone sent me an airplane!"

With trembling hands, she tore the plastic wrap from the box and opened the lid. A sheet of shiny

*50*

paper printed with aircraft markings and a minia-ture representation of an instrument panel lay over a collection of small wood strips and various pieces of plastic. She recognized what would be the front of the airplane, along with a propeller and a set of wheels made from plastic. A long rubber band, detailed instructions, and several folded sheets of white tissue paper completed the list of contents. There was no note, no message, no hint of the sender's identity.

After looking at the outer box again, Jackie con-cluded that it had been mailed directly from the manufacturer. It seemed that someone had placed the order, probably by phone or over the Internet. That person had specified that she, Jackie Ander-son, was to be the recipient of a Piper Super Cub 95 balsawood construction kit.

A warm, comfortable feeling filled Jackie despite the cold winds blowing beyond the windowpane. She felt connected to someone, although she didn't know to whom. Had Sam sent the kit? Or Tina? They were the only two people on earth who knew that she'd become interested in airplanes. Maybe they went together on the project. Whatever the case, one or both of them had cared enough about her happiness to do something. They had included her in the world they loved so much—the world of airplanes and runways, instrument panels and avia-tion fuel. The world of beautiful views and strong, powerful wings that could lift you above the earth—high above its painful memories. She was holding

in her hands evidence that she mattered to someone, somewhere.

Slowly, almost reverently, she placed the bits and
pieces of the construction kit back into the box
and closed the lid. Walking across the room, she
laid the surprise gift on the nightstand beside her
bed. That way, if she awoke during the night, she'd
see it waiting for her; reminding her that she was
important to at least one person in this world. After school tomorrow, she'd start to work on her
wonderful present. Tomorrow, she'd discover what
it took to construct a scale model of a Piper Super
Cub 95. Tomorrow, she'd begin building her very
own wings.

\* \* \* \* \*

"What's that?" Brenda asked in her annoying,
high-pitched voice as she plunked herself down
uninvited beside Jackie in the school lunchroom.
Groups of students hurried past, balancing food
trays in their outstretched hands.

Jackie was holding up a large sheet of paper on
which were printed numerous strange markings
and drawings. "It's none of your business," she said.

Brenda scowled. "Is it schoolwork?"

"No."

"Then you shouldn't be reading it. In case you
haven't noticed, you're at *school.* You're supposed
to do only *schoolwork* here."

Jackie turned in her seat, trying to ignore her
tormentor. "Actually, this is the lunch hour," she

said, "and I'm spending it reading this instead of gorging myself on greasy pizza. So go away, Brenda. Bother someone else for a while."

Brenda lifted her chin. "I can sit wherever I want."

"Fine. Then sit quietly so I can read."

Brenda leaned forward, trying to catch a glimpse of what Jackie was holding. "Did your Aunt Elsa give that to you?"

"No."

"I think your Aunt Elsa is pretty," Brenda said. She ran her fingers through her unruly brown hair, trying to move stray strands of it into place behind her ears. "Some people say I look a little like your aunt. What do you think?"

Jackie glanced at her companion. "You're a spitting image," she mumbled. Then she paused. "As a matter of fact, you even smell like her. You two must buy your perfume at the same garbage dump."

"It's called 'Winter Rose,' " Brenda said with a smug smile. "Only sophisticated women wear it."

"And they sell it to you anyway?"

Brenda frowned. "Of course, you wouldn't know about sophistication, being the daughter of a jailbird and all."

Jackie closed her eyes, trying her best to keep from responding to her companion's cutting words. After regaining her composure, she went back to her reading.

"What *is* all that stuff?" Brenda asked, grabbing

the paper out of Jackie's hands. "Looks like some kind of instructions."

Jackie jumped to her feet. "Give that back!"

Brenda kept her prize out of Jackie's reach as she studied the markings and numbers printed neatly on the surface of the paper. "Hey, these are instructions, like for building something," she announced. Then she flipped the paper over and gasped. "An airplane!" she cried, studying the illustrations that showed how the finished product was supposed to look. "These are instructions for building an airplane!"

"Not a real one," Jackie countered, retrieving the paper from her classmate's grasp. "Just a model. Made from balsawood, if you must know."

"You're building a model airplane?"

"Yes! Now, leave me alone so I can enjoy what's left of my lunch hour. Go put on some more Winter Rose. I don't think they can smell you in Milwaukee yet."

Brenda moved close to Jackie, her face twisted into a scowl. "Sophisticated women don't build airplanes," she whispered. "That's a stupid thing to do." Then she turned and walked away, smiling sweetly at those she passed.

Jackie shook her head and returned to her reading. After a moment, she glanced across the room to where Brenda stood with a gaggle of friends, all of them looking in her direction and pointing between covered-mouth giggles. Surprisingly, Brenda was right. She did look a little like Aunt Elsa. *Great,*

Jackie thought to herself. *Now I get to enjoy my lovely aunt's company all day as well as all night long. What a lucky person I am.*

With a groan of frustration, Jackie continued reading. She was discovering that she'd need to stop by the store on the way home for a few supplies. Building a flyable model airplane was no walk in the park. But she was going to try. After all, one can't fly unless one has wings.

* * * * *

That night, after Jackie had finished her homework, she retrieved her precious box from the nightstand and placed it on her study table. Then she opened the bag of goodies she'd purchased at the store on the way home from school. She was glad that her father, despite his many weaknesses, had been a generous man during the past few years, giving her a hefty allowance week after week and even paying her handsomely for her good grades. She had saved most of this money.

When she'd been forced to move to Wisconsin, she had taken her three-hundred dollars from the Cyprus Hill Savings and Loan and deposited it in the only bank in Lakeside. Now, she was using that money to buy those special things that a girl her age needed to survive in a new environment, like construction supplies for a Piper Super Cub 95 model airplane.

Jackie grinned as she lifted each purchase out of the bag. One roll of waxed paper, one box of straight pins, a tube of wood cement and one of plastic cement, a small box of single-edged razor blades, some fine-grade sandpaper, a small paint brush, and a little bottle of dope from the hardware store. That last item made her laugh every time she saw it. "A little bottle of dope," she giggled aloud. "This is what you'd have if you put Brenda in a jar."

Following the suggestions written on the instruction sheet, she found an empty box out in the garage and cut it open to create a flat cardboard surface big enough to contain the instruction sheet. Then she attached the instruction sheet to the cardboard with tape, and over this she laid a sheet of waxed paper. The drawings and patterns on the instruction sheet showed through the waxed paper, which made a glue-resistant surface on which she could lay the bits and pieces of the aircraft and glue them together.

As she worked, she learned words that she'd never heard before: *fuselage, aileron, horizontal stabilizer, strut.* Apparently, they were parts of an airplane. She did recognize several words: *wings, engine, propeller,* and *cockpit.* Jackie figured that *landing gear* meant what the airplane lands on—the wheel, of course, and the parts to which they were fastened below the main body of the aircraft. Everything sounded so mysterious, so exciting. She was about to create an airplane using the contents of a single box of parts! The thought thrilled her to her very toes.

With the persistent rain still brushing against her windowpane, she went to work. She cut, trimmed, shaped, bent, joined, and glued each piece of balsawood with tender care, treating each delicate structure as if it were made of glass.

*Delicate* was certainly the right word for the wood. It was feather-light and very breakable. Jackie could slice through it easily with her sharp, single-edged razor blade. She wanted to make sure she did exactly as the instructions ordered. So she bent low over her work as she connected each part to the next, slowly forming intricate wooden patterns on the waxed paper.

Jackie wondered how anything so weightless and fragile could stand up to the demands of flying through the air, of following a fast-spinning propeller into the sky. But she knew it would, because the box declared that this was a "flying model." It wasn't meant just to sit on a shelf somewhere. This Piper Cub would beat gravity and lift itself up by its own power.

Jackie hoped to see that happen. She hoped to have the joy of watching this little collection of balsawood, plastic, and tissue rise into the air. It was that hope that kept her fingers moving late into the night, and the next night, and the next. She was determined that she'd bring this fragile craft to life.

# Chapter 5

# Raise Your Right Hand

Sam Fieldstone found himself glancing out through the hangar door in the direction of the driveway every few minutes. For the first time in more than a week the rain had finally stopped, the sun was shining brightly as it sank into the western horizon, and the water that had been standing on his grass runway was disappearing into the soil. By tomorrow, he should be able to tell his customers to come and take delivery of their now mechanically sound aircraft.

Sam didn't want to admit to himself that he'd missed having Jackie around for these past few days. Yes, she annoyed him to no end with her constant talk—asking questions, going on and on about anything and everything. But lately, his place of business had been far too quiet save for the occasional racket of the compressor and pressure tank that drove his pneumatic tools or the hiss of the sandblaster he used to clean spark plugs and assorted engine parts. There certainly was something to be said about peace and quiet. But there was also something to be said about listening to the thoughts and opinions of a twelve-year-old girl who'd recently lost everything she held dear.

Suddenly, a bike and rider appeared, skidding to a stop just outside the hangar entrance. Sam smiled, and then quickly replaced his smile with a scowl. "Not you again!" he called, trying to sound gruff. Jackie slipped around between the parked airplanes and hurried over to him, her cheeks flushed and rosy from the cold air through which she'd just traveled on her way from town. "Raise your right hand," she ordered breathlessly.

"Why?"

"Just raise it!"

Sam complied, lifting his oil-stained right hand, socket wrench held tightly in his fingers.

"Repeat after me."

"Repeat after me."

Jackie paused. "No, not that part."

"No, not that part."

The girl reached up and put her hand over the mechanic's mouth. "Don't say anything until I tell you, OK?"

Sam nodded.

Jackie cleared her throat. "I, Sam Fieldstone . . ." she said. Then she pointed at him.

"I, Sam Fieldstone . . ." he repeated.

"Do hereby join and will serve as a faithful member of . . ."

"Do hereby join and will serve as a faithful member of . . ."

"The Jackie Anderson Honors Club."

The man paused. "The what?"

"The Jackie Anderson Honors Club."

"The Jackie Anderson Honors Club."

Jackie extended her hand. "Welcome, new member. Glad to have you aboard."

Sam shook hands with her and then frowned. "How many people are in this organization?"

Jackie lifted her fingers, as if counting. "Including you and me?" she asked.

"Yes."

"Two."

"And what do members of this club do?"

"Well, for now, we build airplanes."

A wide grin spread across the pilot's face. "You got the kit?"

Jackie pointed at him enthusiastically. "I *knew* it was you! What a great gift, Sam. I've already got the wings finished, except for the tissue covering. And I've started on the fuselage." She motioned toward the main body of an airplane parked nearby. "That's the fuselage, you know. And that's the horizontal stabilizer," she added, indicating the small set of wings at the tail of the aircraft. "That part sticking up—which some people call the rudder—is known as the vertical stabilizer. Those little flaps on the main wings that move up and down when you bank and turn are the ailerons. The pilot sits in what's called the cockpit. And these gizmos here are struts—you know, the bars that hold the wings in place, except for low-wing aircraft like Pipers or Beeches. They don't need external struts. Oh, and the engine makes the propeller go around, and you land on the landing gear. That Cessna 172 airplane out in front of the hangar has fixed gear as opposed to the Piper Arrow over there by the workbench. It's called a retractable—the landing gear folds up into the wings after takeoff."

Sam stood with his bottom jaw hanging limp. "Wow, young lady. That's amazing! How'd you learn all that stuff?"

Jackie smiled. "Well, if you're working on your Airplane Modeling honor, which is what we're doing right now in our Honors Club, you gotta know this stuff. Here, read this." She retrieved a folded sheet of paper from her back pocket and handed it to her friend. "I found it in my Pathfinder handbook and made a copy for you. See? I'm going to do everything it says so I can get my patch. You can get one too, if you want. I borrowed a book from the school library that tells about flying and airplanes and aviation history. Did you know that Charles Lindbergh was the first person to fly solo across the Atlantic? He did it in a single-engine monoplane with fixed gear and no front windshield. He fell asleep and almost crashed into the Atlantic Ocean. Very exciting. Are you hungry?"

Sam blinked. "Ah, sure. Are you?"

Jackie chuckled. "I'm always hungry."

"Well, you're welcome to whatever's in the kitchen."

The girl ran to the small room built into the back of the hangar and then reemerged moments later with a look of astonishment on her face. "Hey, Sam," she called, "where'd you get all this food? There's got to be an entire grocery store in there."

"Tina stopped by yesterday on her way back to Oshkosh. Said she was doing some business up in Green Bay. She must've gone shopping, because the back of her car was loaded down with more food than I've ever seen. She said that a good cook deserves good food, and she hopes you like what she brought."

"Like it? I love it! We could feed an army with what's in there."

"Well, feel free to make whatever you want," Sam said as he tossed a socket wrench into his tall tool chest. "I'm going out to check the condition of the runway before it gets dark. I'll be back in a few minutes. Just make yourself at home in the kitchen." The man walked to a small motorcycle he kept parked by the hangar door, threw his leg over the seat, and pushed the starter button. Jackie watched the motorcycle hurry away, splashing through the puddles still dotting the surface of the ground.

The girl waved and was about to head back to the kitchen when she spotted the closed door behind the battered golf cart. The hangar was silent, save for the distant buzz of Sam's motorcycle as it moved farther and farther away, following the edge of the grass strip.

What was in that room? What waited behind that door? What could have caused her friend to become so angry when she just came close to that mysterious section of the hangar?

Should she look? It was really none of her business. Still, she could tell that whatever was in there caused Sam Fieldstone much anger and grief. She owed it to him to find out, right? That's what friends do, wasn't it? Didn't he listen to her troubles without batting an eye? Didn't he involve himself in her life, trying to make her happy by sending her a Piper Super Cub 95 model to build? Yes, she must see what was in that room because she wanted to return the favor.

With a quick glance toward the field, she hurried over to the door and twisted the doorknob. With a creak, snap, and moan, the door opened, and Jackie stepped inside.

The only light that illuminated what she figured must be a very large room came from the open door. She could make out the dim outline of a desk, a filing cabinet, and what looked like a dust-covered car. The far reaches of the chamber remained cloaked in inky darkness.

A coat rack stood by the door, and from it hung what appeared to be a military jacket, complete with stiff lapels and shiny buttons. Moving closer to admire the garment in the dim light, the girl suddenly stiffened. A dark, ragged stain ran from the neck of the jacket all the way down a sleeve that was torn and almost shredded. A once-proud cap hung atop the rack, its visor ripped and coated with the same dark discoloration. The realization of what it was hit her like a stone. The ugly stain hadn't been made by mud or oil. It had the unmistakable look of dried blood.

Jackie whirled about and exited the room so quickly that she fell over the battered golf cart. Picking herself up, she turned around, grabbed the doorknob, and slammed the door shut. Then she hurried in the direction of the kitchen.

Once in the safety of the well-lit room, she fell onto a chair, her hands trembling, her breath shallow and rough. What was going on? Why was a bloodstained coat hanging in a room that Sam Fieldstone didn't want her to enter? Something horrible must have happened there, something too terrible to imagine. But what?

"Jackie?"

The girl jumped when she heard someone call her name. Bolting from the chair, she tripped over a box of oranges, fell heavily against the bags of groceries on the counter, and slipped to the floor under a cascading flood of produce, boxes, and cans. She saw a flash of light and felt a sharp pain slice through her head. Then all was dark, and she felt as though she were floating through space, drifting among constellations of blue and orange stars. She had no sense of time or place, just a feeling of full release from everything that held her down.

Then, from far away, she heard someone calling her name. "Jackie. Jackie!"

She wanted to respond, but she couldn't speak. All she could do was float.

"Jackie? Wake up. Please wake up!"

The voice sounded worried, urgent, as if someone were in trouble.

"I think she's coming around," she heard yet another voice say. "That was quite a blow to her head. Must've knocked her out."

Slowly, painfully, Jackie opened her eyes to see someone bending over her—a face hidden behind what seemed like a misty veil.

"Creamed corn," she heard the blurry image say. "You got hit on the head by a can of creamed corn."

As the image cleared, Jackie gasped when she recognized the face of Sam Fieldstone hovering over her.

*"No!"* she cried, struggling to back away from the man. *"No!"*

"Jackie, what's the matter?" the other voice called out.

She turned to see Tina kneeling beside the pilot, her normally laughing eyes shadowed with deep concern. Jackie grabbed the woman's arm and pulled her down close to her. "Blood," she whispered. "There's blood on the coat."

Tina glanced around the room and then back at the girl. "What blood, Jackie? What coat?"

Sam stared at the fallen girl who was gazing at him in terror and struggling to move away. "It's . . . it's OK," he said. "She saw the coat."

*"What coat?"* Tina shouted. "Sam, what is she talking about?"

The man lowered himself to the floor as a groan rose from his throat. "She must've gone into the room, the one at the back of the hangar."

Tina studied her friend's face for a long moment. "What's going on, Sam? Tell me what you're talking about, and do it now!"

The pilot nodded. "I'll do better than that. I'll show you. I'll show you both."

Tina helped Jackie to her feet and supported her as the three moved out of the kitchen toward the door behind the golf cart. A tiny rill of blood oozed from the lump atop Jackie's head and moistened her hair. She held on to Tina tightly.

At the door, Sam paused. "I . . . I had a partner many years ago," he said. "We flew together for a charter company based out of Wittman in Oshkosh. I let him live here in an old hangar. I built the new one after . . ."

"After what?" Tina asked.

Sam opened the door, and the three stepped inside. Reaching up, the pilot flipped a switch, flooding a large, open space with light. Tina and Jackie saw that they were standing in a hangar. It was smaller than the one Sam worked in now, but still large enough to house several aircraft and what appeared to be a small apartment. They saw a bed, a nightstand, a work desk and chair, and even an old television set. Off to one side sat a car, its windows, like everything else in the big room, covered with layers of dust.

"We were flying back from Philadelphia," Sam said as he sat down on the edge of the bed, causing the aging springs to squeak. "But we didn't make it. We crashed. And my partner was killed." The man's shoulders sagged under the heavy weight of memory. "I pulled him from the wreckage, but I couldn't do anything for him. He died in my arms."

"It . . . it was an accident," Tina said softly.

"Maybe," Sam responded. "Or maybe I should have known better than to fly in such bad weather. Maybe I should have landed at an airport along the way. Maybe I should have canceled the flight altogether. But I pushed on, saying I could handle it. I was flying the airplane. I was the pilot in command. I was making all the decisions."

Sam paused, reliving in his mind the painful events from the past. "Anyway, I took his coat and cap with me when I left the coroner's office and hung it over there by the door. That's where he always put them when he came in from work. That's where they belonged. And . . . that's where they've been ever since.

"After the funeral, I closed that door. In time, I built the new hangar in front of this one. I made it look like a barn, hoping it wouldn't remind me of what was here before. I left this room and all of its memories behind, sealing it like a tomb—except for that one door. I figured someday I could come back in here. It's been twenty years now." The man turned to face Jackie. "I'm so sorry this frightened you," he said. "You weren't supposed to see it. No one was."

Tina moved to the dusty dresser by the desk and picked up a framed photograph. Pushing aside layers of grime and cobwebs, she noticed two men, one much younger than the other, standing proudly at the nose of a twin-engine aircraft. Both were wearing the crisp, starched uniforms of charter pilots. "What was his name?" Tina asked quietly.

"Terry," came the whispered reply. "Terry Fieldstone."

"Fieldstone?" Jackie repeated hesitantly.

"Yes," Sam answered as he lowered his face into his hands. "I killed my own son."

Tina sat down beside her friend. "I've heard stories," she said. "The guys at Wittman like to hangar-talk—to gossip about the past. I want you to know that nobody blames you, Sam. Nobody says you did anything wrong. It was an accident, pure and simple. Weather is unpredictable. It changes constantly. What's flyable one minute can turn on you the next. Bad weather can become flyable just as quickly. You can't blame yourself, Sam—you just can't. You're a great pilot. Everyone says so. I'd fly with you anywhere. You've got to believe that."

Sam nodded slowly and then rose to his feet. He stood gazing across the large expanse of the old hangar, listening to sounds and voices no one else could hear. "He trusted me," he said. "Terry trusted me, and I let him down. Since that day, I've never taken anyone up with me in an airplane. And I don't intend to ever again."

With that, he walked toward the door and switched off the light, returning the big room and its painful memories to the darkness.

# Chapter 6

# Show and Tell

Jackie stood looking up at the nose of the big World War II bomber, marveling at its powerful form and threatening stance. "What did you say this one was called?" she asked.

Tina stepped out from under the wing and pointed proudly. "This, my friend, is a North American B-25H Mitchell. My grandfather flew one of these in the war. As a matter of fact, B-25s were the first American aircraft to bomb Tokyo after the Japanese attacked our navy fleet at Pearl Harbor. A guy named Doolittle led the raid. They launched these guys off an aircraft carrier, if you can believe it. Gave the enemy a real wake up call. 'Hey, you bomb us? We'll bomb you,' we told them in no uncertain terms."

The two friends strolled to the next aircraft, and the next, enjoying the color and mystery of the EAA AirVenture Museum in Oshkosh. It was their second outing together, and they were having a wonderful time exploring the history of aviation as portrayed by the various displays and the aircraft, large and small, housed in the facility. They sat enthralled in each of the five museum theaters, where stories of aviation creativity and courage flashed on the screens. Jackie even got to "fly" a hang glider down a gently sloping hill in a computer simulation that seemed so real that she screamed when she thought she was going to crash-land on a large rock.

But the highlight of their visit was a ride in a genuine antique aircraft—a Ford Tri-motor owned and operated by the museum. They, along with a handful of other passengers, took off from Pioneer Airport. Old-time hangars filled with old-time airplanes and other aviation-related objects lined one side of this cozy grass strip. As the noisy, all-metal transport rose majestically into the air, everyone inside got a bird's-eye view of Wittman Regional Airport and its collection of large, modern hangars and paved runways and taxiways. At one point, Jackie pointed out the window. "Not long ago, this place was crawling with thirty-two thousand Pathfinders," she told Tina, shouting so she could be heard above the roar and rattle of the three engines. "They had what was called a camporee. I couldn't come, but some in my club did. They said it was awesome."

Tina nodded. "I remember seeing that," she said. "The kids set up camp over there in that huge field. When they all wore their uniforms, it looked as if a bunch of really young soldiers had invaded the airport. It was in all the papers. I'm sorry you couldn't attend."

"Yeah, well, we were having problems at home. That was right when everything started to go bad. Who would have thought that I'd end up here after all?"

Tina smiled. "Well, I'm glad you're here, Jackie. And I'm glad you're enjoying yourself in spite of everything that has happened."

The Tri-motor swept over the flat landscape, getting into position to begin a long final approach back to Pioneer Airport. Jackie studied the distant field, trying to imagine what it was like to be with thousands and thousands of Pathfinders, each of them eager to learn something about aviation and about God.

When the aircraft landed, Jackie and Tina headed back to the museum for one more look at the incredible displays. Jackie also wanted to visit the gift shop, to search for something nice to present to her friend Sam.

"It must be horrible to watch your son die in your arms," she said as she looked through the shelves of aviation books that lined the far wall of the museum store. "I don't blame Sam for being sad and angry."

"Absolutely," Tina responded, leafing through a book on World War II bombers.

Jackie paused in her search. "So, what can we do for him?"

Her companion shrugged. "Be nice to him, I guess. His heart is broken. That's a tough injury to heal."

"But there's got to be something else—something that will make him happy again inside."

Tina thought for a moment. "We could pray for him."

Jackie laughed. "That doesn't work, Tina—trust me. Praying only makes you feel angrier when God doesn't answer you."

The woman moved to the Modern Flight section and picked up a book about fighter jets. "Maybe we're asking for the wrong thing," she suggested. "Maybe we're asking God to fix people our way instead of His way."

"Now you sound like a preacher," Jackie said. "Just pray, and everything will be fine, right?"

"I didn't say that," Tina replied. "God has His own way of doing things, and we may not understand what He's up to. After all, He sees stuff a lot more clearly than we do. Take you, for instance. You got a raw deal at home and got shipped off to a different state. Now you find yourself living with an aunt who isn't exactly kid-friendly. So you might say to yourself, 'Poor me. Life is the pits. I may as well shrivel up and die.' "

Jackie frowned, her back turned to her friend.

"Then," Tina continued, "you run across Sam Fieldstone, a man with a broken heart who needs someone to care about him."

"So?" Jackie said.

"So, you cook him delicious meals and talk to him about anything and everything, and suddenly he doesn't feel so lonely, so forgotten."

The girl turned to face her companion. "You mean God got my parents thrown in jail so I could meet a grouchy old pilot who can't fix a decent meal for himself?" There was a touch of anger in her words.

"No," Tina countered quietly. "I mean that *in spite* of the fact that your parents are in jail and *in spite* of the fact that you live in a state with no curves, God is still with you, helping you find people who are even sadder than you. Jackie, your mom and dad will get out of prison someday. You'll see them again, maybe even try to rebuild a life together. But Terry Fieldstone is dead. All Sam can do is remember . . . and mourn."

The woman moved closer to her friend. "Don't you see, Jackie? God *is* answering your prayers. You needed to matter to someone, to have someone care about you. Well, until your folks are free again, you have Sam, and me, and who knows who else just standing in line to bring you a moment or two of joy. And you, in turn, help us with your smiles and your sense of adventure. That's how God works. Everyone benefits if we let Him be a part of our life and trust Him with all our heart. It's a lesson I'm trying my best to learn as well."

Jackie stood motionless for a long moment, letting Tina's words sink into her troubled mind. Could it be that God did answer prayers, but sometimes in strange, unrecognizable ways? That was a big idea, almost too big to understand. But Tina was right. She had been feeling like she was a part of something again—something warm and worthwhile. It occurred to her that she felt that way the most when she was around Sam or Tina—two people who were dealing with painful memories of their own.

"How about this book?" Jackie asked, holding up an illustrated volume on how to make a home-built aircraft. "Do you think Sam would like it?"

"I know he would, Jackie," Tina agreed, brushing stray strands of hair from the girl's eyes. "You're a good friend to Sam," she said. "He needs you to be his friend. So do I."

"Then I suppose you're expecting a book too."

Tina grinned. "Actually I had my eye on that totally cool poster over there—the one with the Tri-motor on it. It's on sale, you know. Just a buck fifty."

Jackie shook her head. "Man, when God answers prayers, it sure costs you a lot of money."

"Hey, I said it was on sale!"

The two friends gathered up their selections and headed for the cashier. There was still more to see during their special day in Oshkosh, and they didn't want to miss a single moment.

\* \* \* \* \*

As winter continued its relentless approach, touching each Wisconsin pasture, lake, and farm with broad brushstrokes of morning frost, Jackie busied herself with her schoolwork and the construction of her Super Cub 95. She had a new motivation for completing the model. Miss Leyland had announced to the class that in two weeks, her classroom would hold its annual show-and-tell program—a chance for each student to share an item that meant something special to him or her. A finished and completely flyable model airplane would fit the bill perfectly, and Jackie was determined to have her project flight-worthy by that date.

She also continued her research on what made airplanes fly. She understood how they were built. After all, she was building an airplane right there on her desk. She also knew that the engine spun the propeller, which moved the whole airplane forward. But one element had her stumped completely. Birds stay in the air by flapping their wings. Even butterflies flutter their way through the sky. However, an aircraft wing just sits there, stiff and unmoving. So, how can it lift the aircraft into the air?

"Good question," Sam said as he worked deep inside the fuselage of an aging V-tail Beech Bonanza. Jackie could see his feet sticking out of the cockpit entrance.

"I mean," the girl said, addressing the soles of the man's work boots, "even with a helicopter, the wings—or rotor blades as they're called—spin around and around. But just look at this airplane. The wings sit there and do nothing." She thought for a moment. "Maybe it's like when I hold my hand outside a car window. The breeze that hits it from below makes it move up. Is that how it works?"

Sam emerged with a determined look on his face. "Get me the green-handled screwdriver, the one with the paint on it," he instructed. Jackie hurried to the tall, red tool chest and retrieved the requested item. She handed it to the mechanic, who disappeared once again behind the rear seat. "You're on the right track," he said, "but that's only part of the story." His feet jerked and twisted as he worked. "What you're trying to figure out is something called *lift*. Without it, nothing would fly, not even birds."

"How does it work?" Jackie pressed.

She saw Sam's feet hold still for a moment. "Get a clean sheet of paper," he ordered, "like one you'd write on in school."

Jackie obeyed, digging the requested object out of her backpack.

"Tear it in half from top to bottom."

*Rip.*

"Now, use your forefingers and thumbs to grasp one strip by the corners of one of the short edges. Hold it so the short edge rests just below your bottom lip. Are you doing that?"

"Yes."

"Good."

Sam continued working deep in the aircraft as Jackie stood by the wing, a white sheet of paper jutting out from below her mouth and curving down toward her chest like a thin, white beard. She waited . . . and waited . . . and waited.

"Hey, Sam," she called.

"Yeah?"

"Now what am I supposed to do?"

"Oh," the man laughed. "Sorry. I got to concentrating on this frayed cable. Lift. Yes, we were talking about lift. You've got the paper in position?"

"Yes."

"OK, now blow, like you're blowing out the candles on a birthday cake."

Jackie obeyed, and the strip of paper flew up and flapped in the breeze she was creating. Her eyes opened wide. "Hey, the paper came up!" she called. Then she repeated the trick.

"Is there any air pushing it up from below?"

"No. All I'm doing is blowing air over the top of the paper."

Sam wiggled himself out from the fuselage once again and sat by the cockpit entrance. "That's lift. Most of it happens *on top* of the wing. Here, let me show you how it works on this Bonanza." He led Jackie to the far side of the sleek aircraft. "When you look down the top surface of this wing, what do you see?"

Jackie bent over and squinted. "It's . . . it's curved from front to back, like this." She demonstrated with her hand.

"That's right. Now look underneath."

Jackie did so. "Almost flat," she said.

"When the airplane moves forward, the curved surface on top of the wing speeds up the air, kinda like what happens when you squeeze a water hose. The water moves faster as it passes through that squeezed point, allowing you to send a stream out to the flowers at the far end of the flowerbed—know what I mean?"

"Yes."

"Well, as the action of the propeller—that's called thrust—pulls the wing along, this curve speeds up the passage of air over the wing, creating a zone of low pressure. According to the laws of physics, things move from high pressure zones to low pressure zones. So, the wing moves up into that low-pressure zone. The air striking the bottom of the wing helps a bit too, but most of the magic happens up here, on top of the wing. That's lift. That's how airplanes fly. Now, go away so I can get some work done."

Jackie grinned from ear to ear. "Wow. Lift is awesome!" she declared as she blew again and again over her strip of paper, causing it to rise. "I'm definitely going to talk about this at show and tell. The kids in my class will *love* it, and Miss Leyland will think I'm the smartest person in the world. And, you know what, Sam? My Super Cub's wings are curved on top just like the wings of this Bonanza. I glued the tissue on last night and it's shaped exactly the same way. Now I know why."

Sam's shoes kicked as he tightened a screw somewhere deep in the innards of the Beech. "There are no mysteries in aviation science," he called out. "Everything—whether it's a jumbo jet, balsawood model, or mockingbird—follows the same set of rules. Lift is lift."

* * * * *

The big day dawned bright and clear. Jackie was up with the sun, checking and rechecking to make sure that all was ready for her show-and-tell presentation. She even had some surprises planned for everyone and was almost wiggling out of her skin in happy anticipation.

As she sat at the kitchen table enjoying a bowl of cereal—bounty she'd brought with her from her latest visit to Sam's barn—Aunt Elsa entered the room and looked around. "Good morning," Jackie called with a smile. "Fine day, wouldn't you say?"

"It is," the woman responded with more enthusiasm than Jackie had seen from her, well, *ever*. "It's perfect."

"Perfect," Jackie repeated, watching the woman walk around the room and inspect every cupboard as if she were looking for something. "Listen, Jackie," she heard her say. "I won't be here tonight when you come back from school. Something has come up, and, well, I won't be here."

"OK," Jackie said.

"Will you be alright if . . . if I'm not here?"

"Sure. I'll be fine."

The woman smiled. "Great. I knew you would." With that, she turned and left the kitchen. Jackie heard her open the front door and close it quickly behind her. Then all was quiet.

*That woman gets weirder every day,* Jackie thought with a giggle. After all, Aunt Elsa was seldom home when she returned from school. But it was nice of her to let Jackie know that she wouldn't be there this afternoon. The girl smiled. Maybe, just maybe, her dear old aunt was finally growing a heart. Then Jackie turned her early morning musings to the hours ahead, to her upcoming presentation, to the information about flying that she was about to share with her classmates.

\* \* \* \* \*

The playground and front entrance of the school buzzed with activity as Jackie stepped down from the bus. She was holding a big cardboard box that contained her carefully prepared treasures. She saw other classmates similarly burdened, each eager to share the contents of their parcels and containers with their classmates.

The scene was the same in the classroom. Boxes, packages, cages, and even suitcases lined the walls. Their owners sat nearby, offering tantalizing hints about their contents. One particular box housed something that growled. "The ugliest animal in the world," its owner announced, keeping the flaps tightly sealed from prying eyes.

After finding a safe spot for her package, Jackie took her seat and smiled. She knew she had something very special to share. This afternoon's show and tell would be the most amazing event in which she'd ever participated.

Looking around the room, she felt herself relax more than she had for weeks. This was more like it. This was the way it had been in Cyprus Hill.

She loved school. She loved learning things. Now she was going to be a part of the learning process for kids her age. It was an exciting thought, one that stayed with her all morning.

Finally, two o'clock arrived.

Miss Leyland closed her teacher's edition math book and addressed the class. "As you know," she said, "today is show and tell. I can see that you guys are really into it this year. I mean, look at all the boxes and cages and stuff. I'm proud of each of you.

"I've reviewed your items as you listed them on your show-and-tell entry form and have decided the order in which you'll make your presentations. We'll start with Kimberly Mason and end with Jackie Anderson. I'll call your names, and you can make your presentations one by one. Is everyone ready?"

"Ready!" the class chorused eagerly.

"OK. Kimberly, what have you brought for us today?"

A girl with long, blond hair and freckles walked to the front of the classroom and held up a small freezer bag filled with colorful leaves. "My brother and I collected these last week behind our house," she announced. "They are a reminder of autumn, and autumn is my favorite time of year because the trees turn really pretty colors, and the air becomes cool. It also reminds me that Halloween and Thanksgiving are just around the corner. Thank you."

Everyone applauded as Kimberly shyly returned to her seat.

*That was nice,* Jackie thought to herself. *I kind of like autumn, too.*

The next to stand was redheaded and slightly pudgy Jason, who'd brought his pet parrot to school. He gave a short description of the type of bird he held, where it came from, what it ate, and some of the noises it made—especially at two o'clock in the morning, which made his dad throw his slippers at the cage.

So it went, student by student. All had something interesting to say about what they'd brought. Even Brenda sounded surprisingly civil as she showed everyone her makeup kit, complete with eye shadow, blush, and lipstick—examples of which she was proudly wearing as a visual aid. Jackie noticed that all three matched almost perfectly the colors that Aunt Elsa wore each day. *That's totally strange,* Jackie thought to herself. *This girl is like a mini-aunt. Scary.*

Finally, all the students except Jackie had made their presentations. Miss Leyland motioned to her, and Jackie picked up her box and walked to the front of the classroom. "You guys have some really neat stuff," she began. "And I hope you like what I brought to show you."

"Whatever it is, it's stupid," Brenda called from her seat, causing giggles to ripple across the assembled students.

"Keep your thoughts to yourself, Brenda," Miss Leyland ordered firmly. The laughing stopped.

Jackie forced a smile back onto her face. "Recently,

I got interested in airplanes. As a matter of fact, a friend gave me one to build. So I did."

"It's just a model," Brenda sneered. "Anyone can build a dumb model airplane."

Jackie nodded. "Yes. But not everyone takes the time to build one that actually flies." With that, she reached into her box and lifted out a perfectly constructed, perfectly painted, wood-and-tissue model aircraft. All the whispering and mumbling ceased, throwing the room into utter silence. Every eye could see that this wasn't your usual plastic model pieced together in a hurry by some uncoordinated person. This was a work of art—an exact replication of a real airplane. It sported a twenty-four inch wingspan, a clear, plastic windshield, sturdy landing gear, and carefully painted yellow and blue skin highlighted with sweeping curves and expertly applied decals.

Jackie held the craft above her head so all could admire its delicate lines and handsome profile. "This is a model of a Piper Super Cub 95, an airplane design that's been around for many, many years," she announced. "This airplane has been used for civil and military pilot training, crop dusting, aerial photography, cross-country traveling, and even spy work during wars. The real version boasts a 145-horsepower engine. It can travel at 135 miles per hour and fly as high as 13,300 feet."

Jackie identified each part of the craft, pointing out the wings, the stabilizers, the landing gear, fuselage, cockpit, and spinner. Then she smiled and said, "Now, let me tell you about lift." Within minutes, she had everyone in the room blowing over strips of paper dangling from their chins as she explained the simple principles that made it possible for an aircraft to stay in the air.

To conclude her presentation, Jackie told her attentive audience, "So you'll remember what you learned today about airplanes, I have a gift for you." She reached into her box and pulled out stacks of neatly wrapped packages. "These are balsawood gliders—little, easy-to-build airplanes I bought at the AirVenture Museum Gift Shop in Oshkosh. You can put them together really fast and fly them all over the place. It's my way of saying thank you for listening to my speech today."

The room erupted with shouts and applause as Jackie walked the rows, handing glider kits to each student. "Oh," she called over the happy din, "if you'd like, I'll be happy to fly the Cub for you out on the playground. Would that be alright, Miss Leyland?"

The teacher, her face literally beaming with pride, nodded enthusiastically. "I think everyone here would like to see your beautiful airplane fly," she told Jackie. Then, addressing the class, she ordered, "Let's all stand and quietly follow our budding pilot out onto the south recreational field. Remember, there will be no talking until we've exited the building. Other classes are still in session." The students did exactly as they were told, wordlessly following the girl with the handsome model in her arms as she moved out of the classroom and down the empty hallway.

When the string of students reached the soccer field, Jackie lifted her hand. "OK, everyone. I'm going to wind the rubber band really tight so the Cub will give us a good show. You guys stay behind that chalk line there. You're about to see something really cool."

Around and around and around Jackie wound the propeller, twisting the rubber band that stretched between the aircraft's nose and tail inside the fuselage. Then she turned to face the admiring crowd. "OK," she said, "here goes!"

She released her hold of the propeller, and it spun immediately, becoming a blurred circle. Jackie could feel the thrust attempting to pull the airplane out of her hand. Then she gently tossed the craft forward and slightly upward.

The Cub wobbled at first as it picked up speed. Then it settled itself and flew away, rising slowly, majestically over the grassy field. Sunlight sparkled off its broad, outstretched wings, creating a beautiful sheen.

No one spoke. All eyes watched the big model turn slowly, moving in a wide, lazy circle over the field. They could hear the quiet buzz as the spinning propeller whirled through the cold air, pulling the craft higher and higher.

Jackie's precious Cub flew just as perfectly as it had been constructed, moving smoothly through the sky. Unseen forces held it aloft as it drifted effortlessly above the soccer field. This was the proudest moment of her life. It made all the hours and hours of hard work worthwhile.

When the rubber band unwound completely, the propeller stopped, and the airplane's nose pitched down slightly. The craft began to float gently toward the earth thirty feet below. It glided silently, setting itself up for a nice touchdown.

Then a slight breeze stirred, causing the Cub to turn in its descent. It headed directly toward the group of spellbound students. "Everybody just relax," Jackie called out. "The airplane is very, very light and delicate, so don't try to knock it down. Just step aside, and it will fly right past you."

As ordered, the students moved to one side as the Cub slipped past them. Its landing gear brushed the grass, and the airplane bounced slightly before touching down again. As it rolled to a stop, it bumped the ankle of a girl standing near the back of the crowd. "Sorry about that," Jackie called as she hurried through the assembled group, following the course her airplane had just taken.

When she arrived where the Cub rested on the ground, she looked up to see whom it had bumped. Her breath caught in her throat as she gazed into the dark, sinister eyes of Brenda.

"Your airplane attacked me," Brenda said.

"It didn't attack you," Jackie retorted, an uneasy feeling rising in her chest.

"Yes," Brenda countered, her voice toneless and hard, "it attacked me. It's dangerous. And I'm going to do something about that."

Before Jackie could move, Brenda lifted her foot above the fuselage of the delicate airplane. Then she brought it down hard, with a grinding, splintering, tearing *crunch*. In horror, Jackie saw the Cub's wings fold upward, then drop lightly to the ground. "That'll teach you," Brenda said with a scowl. "That'll teach you."

Miss Leyland ran up beside Jackie and stared down at Brenda's right foot, which remained embedded in the twisted, broken remains of the shattered model. Seeing the look in their teacher's eyes, the students ran away, including Brenda. Miss Leyland hurried after them, screaming for everyone to "stop this instant!"

Jackie stood alone on the field, mouth open, tears stinging her eyes, her gaze fixed on the destroyed Cub. "Why?" she whispered. "Why?"

Overcome with sadness, she dropped to her knees before the wreckage. In the distance, the school bell sounded. Classes were over for the day.

# Chapter 7

# A Voice in the Storm

The ride home on the school bus seemed endless. Some passengers in the big, noisy, vibrating vehicle were from Jackie's class and kept their distance, unsure of what to say to their silent classmate. In her lap she held the big box in which lay the remains of her beautiful Cub. Its once-taut covering was torn and twisted, and the delicate balsawood structure forming the fuselage was shattered and crushed. The model's broad wings lay folded, one atop the other, as if trying to hide the horror of its mangled body from prying eyes.

Jackie watched the houses and pastures slip by beyond the window. The sky, which had remained cloudless throughout the day, was beginning to succumb to an approaching storm that was bearing down on Lakeside from the northwest. Some said it might even snow during the night.

When the bus reached Jackie's stop, she slung her backpack on her back, picked up the box, and stepped out into the cold air. She paused long enough at the corner to jam her hands into her thin gloves before continuing up the street toward her house.

Reaching the front door, she dug into her coat pocket for the key. That's when she noticed that the door wasn't closed tightly. She gave it a gentle shove, and it swung open, revealing a front room completely empty of furniture. Jackie shot a quick glance toward the other houses lining the street. She wanted to make sure that, in her confused and saddened state, she hadn't walked up to the wrong door. But, yes, this was her house.

Stepping inside, she noticed that the kitchen, too, had been stripped of everything that could be carried. Jackie pushed open her bedroom door. It squeaked on its hinges as if protesting her unkind act of moving it from where it wanted to be. There, on the floor in the center of the small room, rested her suitcase—the one she'd brought with her from Cyprus Hill. Atop it, tucked under the handle, was a folded piece of paper.

Jackie put down her box and slipped her heavy backpack from her shoulders. She picked up the note and walked to the window, where the last of the fading, late-afternoon light enabled her to read the note:

Dear Jackie,

Bruce has asked me to marry him, and we're moving to Denver, where he hopes to work in the entertainment industry. I've waited a long time for someone like Bruce, and I'm excited about our new life together. I just want you to know that I forgive you for barging into my life like you did. It really wasn't your fault.

As partial payment for my taking care of you for the past several months, I've withdrawn the money from your banking account. As your legal guardian, I'm only taking what's rightfully owed me; I know you'll understand. I also had to sell your bicycle to cover some other obligations. Didn't get much for it, but every little bit helps, right?

One more thing, the house is being rented out first thing tomorrow, so you might want to find somewhere else to stay tonight. You said this morning that you'll be fine without me, and I know you will be. You're a tough kid. Have a good life. I'm so happy.

Aunt Elsa

Jackie stared at the note, her face void of any expression. Everything was gone: her family, her home, her money, her only means of transportation, and her beautiful Super Cub. Outside the window, a freezing rain began to fall as night wrapped Lakeside in a cold, lifeless embrace.

* * * * *

Sam steered his aging Ford pickup truck down the long driveway, squinting out through the frosted windshield. The wiper blades were fighting a losing battle with the wet snow pelting his vehicle, but he didn't care. He'd just returned from town, where he'd deposited his earnings for the month before taking himself out to eat at his favorite restaurant. He'd chatted with an old pilot friend until late into the evening.

Sam smiled to himself. During the past few days, he'd managed to complete work on all of the aircraft parked in and around his hangar. Each had been delivered to or picked up by its grateful owner. Two sights brought joy to the heart of a mechanic: a hangar full of work, and a hangar empty after the work was done.

He eased into his parking spot by the side entrance to the barn and switched off the engine. Pulling his coat collar up around his neck, he stepped out into the icy wind and hurried into the warmth of his hangar home. He was expecting another job—a twin-engine Beech Baron that needed an annual inspection—in about a week. For now, he was looking forward to having some downtime with no responsibilities. He'd decided that he might do a bit of much needed cleaning up around the place. Or he could catch up on some reading. Or maybe he'd rent a few DVDs to watch and turn himself into a couch potato for a couple days.

He fixed himself his nightly cup of hot tea and drank it while picking through the small pile of mail left by the postal carrier. Then he headed for bed, slipping his tired body into the sleeping bag atop his army cot. He liked to tell anyone who wondered about his strange sleeping arrangement, "If it's good enough for our fighting men and women, it's good enough for me."

As Sam lay in the darkness, he listened to the wind howl and the icy rain splash against the roof of his spacious dwelling. *Glad I'm not flying tonight,* he thought to himself. *Even the ducks are walking.*

The single light that he always left on in the kitchen flickered off, casting the hangar into total darkness. *Great,* he thought. *Guess the boys at the power company have their work cut out for them. Bad night to have to track down a blown circuit.* He snuggled further down into his sleeping bag. He had his pot-bellied stove and some dry wood ready and waiting to keep him warm. With that reassuring thought echoing in his mind, Sam closed his eyes and waited for sleep to wash over him.

Amid the whistling wind of the storm and the rattling timbers of the hangar, he heard another sound. It was like the cry of a distant animal; a high-pitched, mournful moan that didn't quite belong with the symphony nature was playing just outside his door.

Sam rose up on an elbow and listened, trying to identify what he was hearing—if he was hearing anything at all. Yes, there it was again—an odd note in the chorus the wind and the rain were generating. He slipped slowly from his sleeping bag and stood in the empty hangar, head cocked to one side, listening, listening. The sound seemed to be coming from beyond the back wall, from the other side of the closed door behind the battered golf cart.

Sam stumbled through the darkness to where his trusty flashlight waited by the hangar door. Following its bright beam, he walked to the back of the empty expanse, until he reached the unused door. There it was again, a plaintive lament heartbreaking in tone and mysterious in origin.

Reaching down, he slowly twisted the knob and opened the door, shining his light into the old hangar. The sound was clearer now, blending with the storm, adding a melancholy harmony to the voice of the wind.

The beam of Sam's flashlight drifted past the abandoned filing cabinet, desk, and dresser until it came to rest on the sagging, dust-covered bed. There appeared to be a bulge in the blankets, and it was from that spot that the sound arose. The pilot's eyes opened wide when he finally recognized what he was hearing.

"Jackie?" he called. "Precious Jackie, what's going on?"

He saw her face emerge from the dusty old sheets. A cry of utter helplessness rose from the girl's half-opened mouth. Sam rushed to her and lifted her into his strong arms. "Jackie," he said, "what's the matter? Please tell me, what's the matter?"

The girl couldn't respond. She could only sob deeply, painfully. She was cold, wet, trembling, stiff, and twisted, as if every muscle were tightened in agony.

Sam carried the sobbing girl out of the musty confines of the old hangar and hurried her to his sleeping bag, quickly pushing her into its warm softness, speaking all the time in a low voice. "It's OK, Jackie. Don't be afraid. I won't let anything happen to you. Old Sam will take care of you."

When Jackie was nestled in the sleeping bag, Sam sat down and lifted her—bag and all—onto his lap. He rocked her slowly back and forth and spoke words of comfort. *She must have traveled through the storm to get here,* he reasoned. Glancing over at the spot where she usually parked her bike, he saw that the space was empty, and his mouth dropped open. "She walked!" he gasped. "This precious girl walked from town through this horrible storm."

"Sam?"

He looked down into the swollen eyes of the girl he was holding. She struggled to speak, her lips pale and trembling. "I hope . . . you . . . don't mind." Jackie swallowed hard, her breathing coming in short, painful heaves "I didn't have . . . anywhere else . . . to go."

"Why, Jackie?" Sam asked, brushing strands of cold, wet hair from her face. "Where's your aunt? Where's Aunt Elsa?"

Jackie coughed violently, and then struggled to speak. "Denver," she said. "She's . . . very happy."

Then Sam understood. Jackie's aunt had abandoned her completely, leaving this sweet, twelve-year-old girl to fend for herself. Anger rose from deep in his chest—rage against the thoughtless act of a selfish woman. "Well, don't you worry about a thing, Jackie," he said, gazing into the fearful eyes of his friend. "You're safe now. I'll take care of you. I promise." He stared into the darkness as he held her. "I'll take care of you," he repeated softly.

After a few moments, he felt Jackie's trembling lessen. Her breathing became more shallow, and her moans ceased. They waited together in the dark, empty expanse of the hangar as the storm raged outside; two lonely people lost in a world of sadness.

\* \* \* \* \*

"Jackie?"

The girl stirred at the sound of her name.

"Jackie. Wake up."

Opening her eyes, Jackie looked into the kind face of Tina. "How do you feel?" the woman asked. "Are you hungry?"

Daylight streamed through the high windows that ringed the hangar's arched roof and illuminated the empty expanse beyond the bed. Jackie stared at the person hovering over her for a long moment and then closed her eyes again.

"That's all she does," Sam said as he sat down at a nearby desk. "She'll open her eyes for a few seconds, but she won't speak."

Tina felt Jackie's forehead with the back of her hand. "She doesn't seem to have a fever. I can't imagine anyone walking through last night's storm with just a thin jacket and a pair of worn-out gloves without catching the mother of all colds. She must have one powerful immune system."

Sam nodded. "I'm sorry I had to call you, Tina, but I didn't know what to do for her."

The woman waved her hand. "It's OK, Sam. You did exactly what you should have done. And I would've been here sooner, but they had to clear the roads first. Nothing like six inches of icy slush to keep you off the highway. Oshkosh is a mess, too."

"So, what should we do now?" Sam asked. "She won't eat. She won't talk. It's like . . . it's like she's given up or something."

Tina sighed. "Well, I don't blame her. Poor kid. Her whole world has been snatched away. She's lost everything."

"She hasn't lost us," the pilot announced resolutely. "We're still here."

Yes," the woman agreed. "But I've been with this girl enough to know her pretty well. That tough skin of hers is an act, a defense. With all her confidence and bravado, it's sometimes hard to realize that she's just a young girl lost in a big, frightening world. I'm amazed that she's done as well as she has."

Sam frowned. "What can we do to help her?"

Tina thought for a moment. "All I know," she said, "is what worked for me. I kind of lost everything, too—at least, everything that I thought was important to my life: my husband, my self-respect, my big dreams."

"What did you do?"

The woman smiled. "I found something else to live for."

"What?"

She pointed upward. "The sky. Flying. Getting into an airplane, and sailing off to who knows where, not knowing what I'd find when I decided to land. I also discovered that in the sky, nothing came between God and me. I could talk to Him, scream at Him, cry my silly eyes out and know that no one could see or hear me except Him."

Sam stood and walked to a battered cardboard box resting on a worktable and lifted out the shattered remains of Jackie's Cub. "Do you think that's what she was trying to do with this?" he asked. Tina gasped when she saw the pile of twisted balsawood and torn tissue. "This is the model I sent her a while back," the man continued. "She told me that after she finished building it, she was going to take it to school for some show-and-tell program. That kid did a beautiful job of putting this thing together. I mean, look at the detail work here on the tail and how she attached the nose assembly so perfectly. It's obvious she took pride in her work. This airplane must have been very important to her." He paused as he studied the mangled object he held in his hands. "This model didn't crash. Someone crushed it."

Tears moistened Tina's eyes as she looked down on the broken and twisted Cub. "Oh, Jackie," she whispered. "Who would do this to you?"

The two turned and gazed over at the still form lying in Sam's sleeping bag on the low army cot. They saw clearly now that their friend had, in reality, lost everything she cherished in life. They understood that in her mind, she had no reason to take another breath.

\* \* \* \* \*

*Tap, tap, tap.*

The sound drifted through Jackie's half-asleep mind.

*Scratch, scratch, bang, bang.*

She opened one eye, and then closed it again.

*POUND, POUND, POUND!*

Jackie sat up with a start, a frown shadowing her face.

*Wheeeeee, chick, chick, zip.*

A machine somewhere was running, sending out an irritating rattle.

*Zip, zip, clunk, clunk, BANG!*

"Hello?" the girl called in a husky voice, her greeting echoing about the empty hangar.

*Whirrrrrrrrrr.*

The sounds weren't coming from the usual place. She'd heard most of them before as she'd sat and watched Sam breathe life back into damaged or rough-running aircraft. But the hangar in which she lay contained no such machines—and no mechanic for that matter.

*Rrrrooooaarrrrr, chug, chug, chug, spiffffffffffffff.*

"Sam? Hey, Sam, where are you?"

*Zip, zip, clunk, clunk, BANG!*

Odd. A whole lot of noise, but no one making it. Jackie pulled her feet out of the sleeping bag and placed them on the rug by the cot. That's when she noticed a thick, warm-looking blue coat hanging from the back of a nearby chair. She saw that someone had attached a note to its shoulder. Stumbling across the floor, she picked the coat up, studied it thoughtfully, and decided it was exactly her size. A pair of lined leather gloves lay by the calculator. She also saw the soft folds of a new silk scarf and the bumpy softness of a pair of earmuffs. Insulated knee-high boots stood on the floor.

Jackie removed the note attached to the coat and angled it so the afternoon light filtering in through the high windows would illuminate the handwritten words. "A little something to wear," it read, "just in case you decide to go for another cross-country stroll during an ice storm."

Jackie fought the urge to grin.

*BANG, BANG, BANG, BANG!*

"OK," she called out. "Enough with the banging!" No one answered—because, as she'd discovered, no one was in the hangar. Then she realized that the sounds seemed to be coming from *behind* the hangar, in the direction of the door beyond the golf cart.

"Sam?" she called as she moved around the cart and stood in front of the door. "Sam?"

*Whirrrrrrrr.*

Slowly, she pushed the door open. The old hangar was bathed in light. Someone had swept the floor clean, and the musty furniture and bed were gone. Gone, too, were the coat rack and the soiled garments that had hung on it for so long.

A tall canvas curtain separated the expanse of the old hangar into two sections, a detail she hadn't noticed during her visits into the darkly lit, forbidden space. The noises came from behind the canvas partition.

"Hey, Sam," she called again. "Are you back there?"

"No," a familiar voice responded. "I'm in town eating a burrito."

Jackie chuckled and then cleared her throat. "What are you doing? Don't you know that the owner of this place is a total grouch and doesn't want anyone nosing around in his old hangar?"

"You're right," another voice, this one female, called back. "He *is* a total grouch, especially if you don't give him the right tool."

"Tina?" Jackie said in surprise. "Are *you* here?"

"No," came the quick reply. "I'm in town eating a burrito, too."

Jackie lifted her hands. "What's going on? And why are you guys making so much noise?"

The two emerged from behind the partition, their faces, arms, and work clothes streaked with grime and grease. "Oh, did we wake you?" Tina called, feigning sympathy. "We're so sorry. We all know how important it is for a growing girl to sleep for three days straight."

"I've been sleeping for three days?" Jackie gasped.

"Snoring too, I might add," Sam interjected. "How such a small person can generate such a big snore is beyond me. We had to come out here for some peace and quiet."

"I don't snore!" Jackie countered. Motioning toward the partition, she asked, "So, what are you guys working on? Is your Skylane giving you more trouble, Tina?"

"Nope."

"New customer?"

Sam shook his head. "Nope."

"Do you two just like making noise?"

Tina and Sam grinned. "If it serves a purpose," the woman said.

"Well," Jackie snorted, "you woke me up, that's for sure."

"That was one of the purposes."

The girl frowned. "OK, what's going on? You guys are up to something, and whatever it is, it's behind that big curtain. Right?"

"Right."

"So, what is it?"

Tina walked over to her friend. "Oh, nothing much. Just trying to rebuild something that got crushed."

With that, Sam grabbed one end of the cloth partition and began pulling. The curtain folded onto itself again and again as Sam pulled it across the broad expanse. A high wing appeared, followed by a strut and landing gear. Then a pointed spinner and freshly painted propeller caught the sunlight flooding in through the open hangar door, and another landing gear, strut, and wing made their appearance. Jackie's mouth dropped open, and her breath caught in her throat. "My Cub!" she breathed. "That's my Piper Cub— only bigger!" She glanced at Sam and then back at the aircraft. "It's just like my model. Same color and everything!"

"It belonged to my son," Sam said quietly. "He was in the process of rebuilding it when . . ." The man paused. "He was almost done, too. Kept it right here in the hangar, and worked on it evenings, weekends—whenever he had time. Tina and I figured that it had sat here long enough. I decided that this hangar had been closed up long enough, too."

Jackie walked over and placed her hand on one of the smooth wing struts. "Oh, it's beautiful," she whispered. "Just beautiful."

"So was your model," Sam said. "I'm proud of you, Jackie. We both are. That's what made me decide to open this place up again and to accept the fact that my son is gone." The man cleared his throat before continuing. "You showed me that beauty doesn't just happen. You gotta work at it and not give up." He wiped his hands on an old rag hanging from his pocket. "What happened, Jackie? What happened to your Cub?"

The girl looked down at the floor. "Brenda, a girl in my classroom, crushed it," she said. "She just smashed it with her foot. When I got home, I found that my aunt had left me alone in our empty house. She just left. Sold my bike, took my money, and went off to Denver." Jackie looked over at her friends, her eyes filling with tears. "Why did they do that? Why?"

Tina wrapped the girl in her arms. "I don't know, Sweetheart," she said softly. "But you're not alone anymore. You've got Sam and me. We're not going to leave you. We're not going to take anything away from you. We're not going to crush your dreams. In fact, we're helping you build a new one. See, you have your airplane back. And this one can take you with it when it flies. You can soar above the clouds and sail away to your heart's content. Then, when you're ready, it will bring you back home again."

The woman lifted Jackie's chin and gazed into her eyes. "Jackie," she said, "you can start learning all about aviation right now. There are books to read, like the ones at the AirVenture Museum, re- member? And I know a flight instructor who can start giving you lessons—real flying lessons. When you hit your sixteenth birthday, you can solo and fly all by yourself."

Sam walked up beside his two friends. "Tina has agreed to buy this Cub," he said. "She also wants you to come live with her in Oshkosh—at least until your parents are released from jail. I called your friend Sheriff Curtain in Cyprus Hill, and he's going to work everything out for us. Would you like that?"

"I'm going to live with you, Tina?" Jackie said hesitantly, struggling to believe what she just heard. "Honestly?"

"Honestly," the woman responded, "but you have to stop snoring."

"Can we come and visit Sam?"

"Anytime you like. Besides, somebody's gotta keep our beautiful Cub in good working order, right?"

Jackie's face relaxed into a broad grin. "Right."

Tina hugged the girl tightly as tears stung her eyes. "So, Future Pilot, you have to start eating food and building back your strength. After that, we can make the move to Oshkosh. I have some things to work out at my apartment, and I have to find a good school for you. That shouldn't take more than a week or so. Until then, you can stay here with Sam and help him put the finishing touches on our Cub. I've called your school in Lakeside and informed them that you're moving. Your teacher, Miss Leyland, told me to tell you how sorry she was about the model and that she'll miss you very much. But she said she understands, OK?"

"OK."

Tina slipped out of her stained coveralls and walked to the broad door. "And you, Sam Fieldstone—don't you go making her fix all the meals while I'm gone. She's not your slave."

The man spread his arms in a gesture of defense. "Hey, I did just fine before she showed up. I think I'll be able to keep her alive for a few days."

Jackie dropped to her knees, hands folded in front of her. "Tina," she cried out in a pleading voice. "Don't leave me here. I saw what he used to eat. I'll be dead by tomorrow!"

The woman laughed. "Take good care of our Cub," she ordered.

With that, she turned and walked through the open door of the old hangar. There was a lightness in her step and a joy in her heart that she hadn't felt for a very long time.

Over the course of the next few days, Jackie's strength—both mental and physical—continued to build. She busied herself helping Sam with the Cub, handing him screwdrivers, wrenches, and various other tools much as a surgical nurse hands a doctor his scalpels, clamps, and sutures. Each time she glanced up at the perfectly formed fabric wings above her or gazed down the wood-framed fuselage, she had to pinch herself to prove she wasn't dreaming.

Because of her conscientious work on the model, she recognized much of what she saw in the real airplane. As she helped Sam put the finishing touches on the Super Cub, she felt as though she was rebuilding an old friend, putting back together something she thought she'd lost forever.

\* \* \* \* \*

As the sun began to set on the fourth day of her recovery, yet another winter storm threatened eastern Wisconsin. Angry clouds advanced from the northwest, and the radio weather reporter warned of unsettling winds and icy snows. "We'd better keep the hangar doors closed tightly," Sam announced as he and Jackie surveyed the approaching weather. "I've seen these kinds of blows before. They can mess up a sky like a flood messes up the land."

Jackie nodded. Already the first frigid breath of air generated by the cold front was washing across the landing strip and trying to sneak its way through the new coat she was wearing. And snowflakes had begun drifting in the air like lost children searching for a place to hide.

However, when they closed the hangar doors and lit a fire in the pot-bellied stove by the kitchen, all uncertainty about the weather vanished. It really didn't matter what happened beyond the tightly constructed walls of Sam's barn. Mother Nature could rant and rave all she wanted. For Sam and Jackie, the storm would just be a rattle in the rafters and a soft pounding against the broad doors. They were safe from the elements and had plenty of food to enjoy in the cozy kitchen.

Sam was continually surprising Jackie with his cooking skills—a talent that hadn't been at all evident when she first stared into his almost-empty refrigerator. "I never had cause to fix fancy dishes," he said whenever she complimented him on his latest version of rice and beans, vegetable stew, or cooked cereal. "Besides, Tina will have my hide if I don't load you down with proper nutrition."

This night, as the storm swept across the Wisconsin flatlands on its way east, the two enjoyed a supper of hot bean soup, generous slabs of whole-wheat bread smothered with all-natural grape jelly, and tall glasses of creamy white milk. Sam even produced a box of store-bought chocolate-chip cookies for dessert.

After supper, Jackie ventured out to see what nature was doing to Sam's airport property. The view was shocking. Three inches of snow carpeted the ground, and the wind moaned among the barren, ice-laden tree branches like a wounded animal. Jackie was about to turn around and make her way back toward the hangar when, through the gathering darkness, she saw a flickering light moving along the distant highway.

Suddenly, the light stopped, and a shrill, faint voice called through the groaning winds. "Jackie. Jackie Anderson. Come here!"

Jackie squinted, trying to see through the blowing snow. "What?" she called.

"Come here this instant. Do you hear me? I want to talk to you!"

Jackie's eyes opened wide as she recognized the source of the mysterious summons.

Sam, who'd also heard the call, stepped out of the hangar door and ambled up beside Jackie. He stared toward the road and the distant light. "Who's that?" he asked, trying to rub warmth into his unprotected arms.

"It's not fair," the person shouted angrily, trying to be heard across the distance. "It's all your fault, and you're going to pay."

"What's all your fault?" the man asked, glancing down at Jackie. "What's going on?"

Jackie shook her head and pointed. "Sam Fieldstone, meet Brenda."

"Brenda?" the man gasped. "You mean the girl-who-crushes-model-airplanes-with-her-foot Brenda? What does she want?"

"I don't know," Jackie said, zipping up her warm coat and pulling the leather gloves from her pockets. "I think it's time I find out once and for all."

With that, she started walking across the drifting snow toward the light and the angry girl who waited in the gathering storm.

# Chapter 8

# Mayday

A car moved along the icy highway, following the bright beams tossed forward by its headlights. As Jackie scrambled up a rise onto the shoulder of the road across from Brenda, the car slipped between them, its tires fighting for traction.

"What are you doing here?" Jackie called to Brenda through the wind and blowing snow.

"I live just down the road," Brenda shot back angrily. "I have just as much right to be here as you do."

"OK," Jackie responded, turning to leave. "You have a nice evening."

"You and that dumb airplane of yours got me suspended from school. And you sent her away," Brenda said, her words thick with rage. "It's all your fault."

"Sent who away? Brenda, what are you talking about?"

"Your Aunt Elsa. She left because of you!"

"My aunt left because she fell in love with some guy named Bruce," Jackie said with a chuckle.

"They're in Colorado, if you'd like to visit them. Take money. They'll probably need some."

Brenda's eyes narrowed. "Now your sweet aunt won't be around to tuck you in at night," she said. "I bet you're sorry about that."

Jackie threw up her hands. "Tuck me in? Aunt Elsa? Believe me, there was no tucking. She's not a tucker."

"That's because you weren't kind to her. You didn't treat her right."

Jackie gasped. "I didn't treat *her* right? Brenda, for your information, my Aunt Elsa is a terrible person—a selfish, mean woman who thinks only of herself."

*"That's not true!"* Brenda shouted, shaking her fist in the air. "She's a wonderful lady filled with love and gentleness. I've seen her. She wouldn't have left unless you drove her away. That's what happened, isn't it? You drove her away because you were too demanding, too mean to her."

Jackie stood for a long moment, trying to understand why her crazy classmate cared that her self-centered aunt had decided to pick up and leave for Denver. "What's it to you?" she asked. "She's *my* aunt, not yours."

"You're right," Brenda shot back. "She's not my aunt—she's my *mother.*"

Jackie blinked. "Your what?"

"My mother."

"Brenda, you're totally insane. I've seen your mom and dad. They drop you off at school every day. They drive a green SUV and look like really nice people."

"Those are my adoptive parents," Brenda retorted. "They took me when my birth mother couldn't take care of me anymore. It wasn't her fault. I cried too much. I made her work too hard. I don't blame her for what she did."

Jackie stood unmoving, staring at the defiant girl standing across the road from her. She didn't know what to say. It didn't surprise her that her Aunt Elsa had given birth to a child. It also didn't surprise her that she had given the child up for adoption. "Why didn't you tell me? Why didn't you say something before?"

"I'm not supposed to know about her," Brenda said bitterly. "One day I was looking through some of my dad's stuff, and I found my file. Yes, I have a file. There it was in black and white: names, dates, adoption notification, lawyer reports, everything. Then you come along and start living with her— my own mother. You're with her every day. That should have been me! I should have been living with my mother. You were getting all the love that rightly belongs to me!"

Jackie shook her head. "Brenda, there was no love. Honestly. Your mother, my aunt, doesn't love. She's mean and heartless."

"*You're lying!*" Brenda screamed, "My birth mother is kind and sweet." Brenda took a step forward. "She would sing to me at night if she could. She'd listen to me and tell me how proud she is of me." Brenda's rage intensified as she continued moving slowly in Jackie's direction. "You chased her away. It's all your fault. I hate you. *I hate you!*"

Brenda began running across the road, straight at Jackie. As Jackie turned to escape the attack, she saw a car emerge from the blowing snow, wheels locked, sliding sideways across the icy surface. Before she could yell a warning, she heard a scream and a stomach-churning *thud.* And then all was quiet, except for the howling of the wind.

The car door opened, and a man wearing a business suit scrambled out. "I couldn't stop!" he cried out. "I saw her, and I couldn't stop."

Jackie glanced around. Brenda was gone. The road was empty except for the car and its driver. Then she saw a movement in the tall weeds by the road—a bare hand waving drunkenly in circles. "Brenda!" Jackie shouted, running toward the spot where the girl lay in the broken, icy vegetation. "Brenda, are you alright?" Brenda's hand fell limply onto her motionless, snow-covered body. Her flashlight lay by her face, illuminating her swollen eyes, deathly pale skin, and bloodstained lips.

*"Help!"* Jackie screamed, turning to face the distant barn. "Sam, *help!*" She knelt beside the still form. "Brenda. Brenda! Can you hear me?" But the girl didn't move.

The driver stood by his car, hands over his face. "I didn't mean to hit her. I couldn't stop. I just couldn't." He paused. "We've got to get her to a doctor! But the roads—they're not passable now.

They're full of ice and snow. What are we going to do? What are we going to do?"

At that moment, Jackie heard a familiar sound in the distance. It was the *chung, chung, chung* of an aircraft propeller turning around and around as the starter tried to bring the engine to life. Then she heard a roar. She glanced in the direction of the barn and saw the Super Cub moving in their direction. Its wheels were blasting through the fallen snow, and its propeller was stirring up a blizzard of white. The aircraft taxied quickly across the end of the field and spun around as it approached the road.

Sam set the hand brake and left the engine idling as he opened the door and stepped out into the frigid air. "Let's get the girl into the airplane," he shouted to the driver. "And be careful. We have to keep her back and neck as straight as possible."

The man nodded, and they hurried over to the fallen girl. Gently, they lifted Brenda's limp body, carried her across the icy road, and made their way gingerly onto the field. "We'll put her inside, behind the pilot seat," Sam said. "Let's put her in feet first, with her head by the door." Then Sam ordered, "Get in, Jackie, and hold her head and shoulders on your lap. I'll secure you both after you're settled."

Jackie squeezed herself behind the pilot seat and sat facing the tail of the aircraft on the narrow, wood floor. Sam had yet to install the back seat in the Cub, so there was just enough room for her and the injured girl. Jackie looked down at Brenda's pale face as Sam tightened the seatbelt around them. Then he settled into his seat and slammed the door closed. "Hang on!" he shouted.

Jackie heard the engine roar to full throttle as the craft lurched forward. They sped across the dark, snow-covered field and rose into the air. She glanced out the window by her head and gasped when she saw how quickly they were moving over the ground. Treetops rushed by almost within reach as the Super Cub turned eastward, chased by the storm.

Sam's hands moved quickly from throttle to trim to mixture control as he set the aircraft up for fast cruise. A thick layer of icy clouds hovered just above the airplane, keeping him from climbing more than a few hundred feet above the ground as they sped over the flat Wisconsin landscape. Through the horizontal flow of snow, he could see dimly lit farmhouses and dark pastures move by under the plane's outstretched wings. "We're heading straight for Lake Michigan," he called above the roar of the engine and the rush of the wind. "Then we'll turn south and hug the shoreline. There won't be any obstructions in our way once we're over the water."

"Where are we going?" Jackie shouted.

"Milwaukee," came the quick reply. "They've got a pediatric hospital with a trauma ward near the General Mitchell International Airport." Reaching down, he added, "I'm going to try to contact someone on this old radio. I have no idea if it still works, but it's all we've got."

With that, Sam switched on the bulky transceiver mounted below the instrument panel and waited while its ancient tubes warmed to life. He dialed in 121.5, the universal emergency frequency for all aircraft. "Mayday, mayday," he called into the microphone, "this is Piper niner four one two papa. Do you read? Over." Static crackled from the tiny speaker mounted just above his head. "Mayday, mayday," he repeated. "Piper niner four one two papa broadcasting in the blind on one twenty one point five. Does anybody read me? Over."

Static. Then, "Aircraft calling on one twenty one point five, this is Chicago Center. What is your location and type of emergency? Over."

"Chicago, Piper niner four one two papa is approaching the shore of Lake Michigan in the vicinity of Manitowoc. I'm flying low in marginal weather and will be heading south to Milwaukee. We're not instrument equipped, and I am squawking one two zero zero. I've got an injured child who's been struck by a car. Total souls on board are three. Request flight following and airspace clearance. Over."

"Roger that, one two papa," came the instant reply. "Squawk seven seven zero zero and ident. Say type of aircraft."

Sam dialed in the requested numbers on his transponder and pushed the ident button. "We're a Piper Super Cub with three hours fuel," he said into the microphone. "I'm estimating Mitchell in forty-five minutes."

After a few moments of silence, the radio crackled to life again. "One two papa is radar contact over Manitowoc. You can update that estimate. Winds along your route are northerly at forty knots! That should put you into Mitchell in about thirty minutes. We're contacting Memorial Hospital in Oak Creek, and they'll have equipment and trauma personnel waiting on the runway when you land. Remain on this frequency. Over."

"Roger that," Sam responded with a great sigh of relief. "Thanks, guys."

"You're welcome, Sam," came the warm reply.

Sam banked the airplane hard right as it swept out over the shoreline of Lake Michigan. Soon they were racing south, following the dim line of the waves washing against the beach just a few hundred feet below. Their little craft bumped from side to side and up and down as the storm pushed it faster and faster.

Jackie looked down at the silent passenger whose head and shoulders lay cradled in her lap. As much as she didn't like Brenda, she couldn't help but feel sorry for the girl. Here was someone who, like her, felt lost and abandoned—a person separated from her birth mother and unable to share her broken heart with anyone. That's why she'd been so mean, why she carried such hatred in her heart. As strange as it seemed, Aunt Elsa was an important part of this girl's life. She was her only link to her past, to the generations who'd come before. Brenda's longing for her mother was more than a simple curiosity about who'd given her birth. Elsa was her only connection to who she really was and who she'd become someday.

"You're not going to believe this," Jackie called over her shoulder.

"Believe what?"

"This Brenda, this royal pain who enjoys making my life miserable, this evil smasher of model airplanes, is my cousin."

"Your *cousin?*"

"Yup. Her birth mom is none other than dear ol' Aunt Elsa. Is that totally weird or what?"

The Super Cub bounced through rough air as Sam fought to keep the wings level. "Are you sure she's telling you the truth?"

Jackie nodded. "Trust me; this has *got* to be her daughter. They even smell alike. Besides, Brenda has seen the legal documents that name Aunt Elsa as her birth mother."

The girl in Jackie's lap stirred, a low moan escaping her swollen lips. "She's waking up," Jackie called. "What should I do?"

"Try to keep her calm," Sam replied as he strained to see through the rushing cascade of snow. "She may have serious internal injuries that we don't know about. Tell her to stay still."

Brenda's eyes fluttered open, and she stared up at Jackie for a long moment. Then, suddenly, she tried to squirm away while screaming out, "What are you doing? Where am I?"

Jackie held her down tightly. "You got hit by a car, and we're taking you to the hospital," she said. "You have to lie still, Brenda. You might be hurt bad inside, and you shouldn't move."

"Don't you tell me what to do!" Brenda shouted, struggling to escape Jackie's tight hold. "I don't want your help. Let me out of here this instant." She unfastened the seatbelt that was holding her down and started pounding on the frosted windows with her fists. "Let me out. LET ME OUT!"

"What should I do?" Jackie shouted. "She's losing it."

Sam reached over and flipped open the window beside him. A blast of frigid air rushed past his shoulder and hit the struggling girl like a frozen sledgehammer. Brenda stopped her thrashing as she suddenly found herself staring down at the dark, cold waves hundreds of feet below. "Where am I?" she screamed, grabbing Jackie by the shoulders. "What are you doing to me?"

"We're taking you to a hospital in Milwaukee," Jackie shouted, trying to be heard above the roar of the wind. "The roads are closed because of the storm, so my friend Sam is flying us there. Now, lie down and be quiet!"

Brenda's eyes opened wider and wider as she glanced wildly about. She saw the wings, the thick struts, and the soft swirl of the propeller spinning out in front. A look of confusion and terror filled her face as she stared at Jackie. "This looks familiar," she said, in an almost pleading tone. "Why does this all look familiar?" She coughed violently as fresh blood moistened her lips and ran down her chin. "I'm afraid, Jackie. I'm afraid!"

Jackie pulled the trembling girl down onto her lap. "Brenda, you'll be OK if you just lie still. I'll take care of you. After all, you're my cousin. We're . . . family. And family members take care of each other, right?"

Brenda stopped struggling. "You're my cousin," she repeated as if realizing that fact for the first time. "Yes. You're my cousin." She allowed herself to relax against Jackie's stomach and chest as she felt her warm arms encircle her. "Don't leave me, Jackie," she whispered. "Please, don't leave me."

"I won't," Jackie promised. "But you've got to lie still so Sam and I can get you to the hospital. Just don't move, OK?"

Brenda coughed again and nodded slowly. She remained motionless as the airplane pounded through the rough air, heading south along the shoreline. Up ahead, the lights of Milwaukee's northern suburbs were beginning to emerge from the blinding snow and slip by under the aircraft's right wing. Sam spoke with the controllers who were following his flight. They told him that all was ready for their arrival at the big airport south of the city. "Use any runway that works for you," they said.

"Do you hate me?" a thin, wavering voice called in the darkness. "I wouldn't blame you if you did."

Jackie shook her head. "No, I don't hate you, Brenda. Can't say as I like you very much, though."

"Am I going to die?" the girl asked, flinching as a sudden pain seared her midsection. Her hand tightened around Jackie's arm.

"Sam is flying as fast as he can," Jackie said as she turned and glanced out the window. "I can see lights below. We're almost there. Just lie still a few minutes more."

Brenda listened to the sound of the engine and the chatter coming from the radio. When she spoke, her words were heavy and strained. "Why are you doing this for me? I was trying to hurt you."

"I'm not like you," Jackie said coldly.

Sudden sobs shook the injured girl, causing her to double over in pain. "I don't want to be like me either," she groaned. "I don't want . . ." Her body went limp.

*"Sam!"* Jackie screamed. *"Hurry. Please hurry!"*

The pilot lowered the nose of the Super Cub and pushed the throttle full forward. Up ahead, he could see the flashing lead-in lights of runway one nine right at General Mitchell International Airport. Milwaukee shone through the falling snow, casting an eerie glow on the bottom of the thick cloud layer just above their wings. "I have the airport in sight," he shouted over his shoulder, reaching for the microphone. "We'll be down in just a few minutes. Hang in there, Jackie!"

In the distance, the runway waited. An ambulance filled with lifesaving equipment and the skillful hands the injured passenger needed so desperately sat at a taxiway intersection. Jackie closed her eyes. "Fly," she said softly. "Fly fast, Sam. Fly fast!"

# Chapter 9

# Spring

Jackie sat on a log by the grass strip watching Tina fly the Super Cub around and around and around the traffic pattern of Sam's little country airport. A breeze was blowing, warm and inviting, from the west, scented by the wildflowers growing along the highway.

The winter had been long and hard, filled with howling winds and drifting snows. Now, those months were fast becoming a fading memory, as Wisconsin residents emerged from their cold season, rejuvenated and eager for spring.

"What do you think?" Sam asked as he lowered himself down beside Jackie.

"Looks good to me," Jackie said, watching the aircraft fly the downwind leg, its bright yellow wings shining in the sunlight. "She's got good speed control and flies a tight pattern. Even did a wheel landing on her last pass. Impressive."

"She's a natural," Sam said with a smile. "That woman belongs in the air." He snapped his fingers. "Oh, I almost forgot. This came for you last week."

He handed Jackie an envelope. "It's addressed to the president of the Jackie Anderson Honors Club. Since I'm only a lowly member of that solemn organization, not the president, I figure it's probably for you."

The girl grinned broadly. "I bet I know what this is," she said, tearing the envelope open. Inside she found a note handwritten by her old Pathfinder leader, Mr. Cho.

Dear Jackie,

Congratulations on completing all of the requirements for your Airplane Modeling honor. Both you and your other member should be very proud of your accomplishment. Tell Sam he seems to me to be a fine young fellow, and I'm sure he has a bright future waiting for him in aviation. Enclosed you'll find your Airplane Modeling patches. Again, congratulations, and God bless you both. We miss you.

Mr. Cho.

Jackie chuckled as she withdrew two small, oval patches with the image of an airplane sewn into them. "Mr. Cho says you have a bright future waiting for you in aviation," she declared as she handed Sam his colorful badge.

"Thanks," Sam said with a satisfied smile. "Hey, the plane on here looks just like a Super Cub."

"Yeah," Jackie agreed. "It sure does."

The two sat in silence as Tina drifted in for another touch and go. They waved as she roared past and lifted into the air again.

"What do you hear from Brenda?" Sam asked as he watched the beautiful aircraft climb above the trees at the far end of his property.

"She hates the wheelchair," Jackie said. "Says it gets in the way when she's playing soccer." The girl paused. "But she did say some guy named Andrew keeps offering to push her around between classes."

"Sounds like love is in the air," Sam declared. "Just proves that there's somebody for everyone."

"I write to her once a week," Jackie said. "After all, she's the only blood family I've got out here in the flatlands. Oh, and I got a letter from my mom last week. She said she'll be coming up for parole in five years instead of six. That's good news."

"Sure is," Sam encouraged.

The girl sighed. "You know what?"

"What."

"The pastor at my church in Cyprus Hill was right. He said that when everything is bad, God is hard at work making a way for things to get better. He said God has people just waiting to pick you up if you fall. That's exactly what happened to me. You and Tina became my friends just when I needed you most."

Sam smiled. "That worked both ways, Jackie," he said. "We needed someone like you in our lives, to help turn our focus away from ourselves and all of our troubles. This God of yours is pretty smart.

I'd like for you to tell me more about Him sometime."

The Super Cub drifted toward the grassy runway and touched down feather-light. Tina taxied over to where the two waited and shut down the motor. "I *love* this airplane," they heard her shout as she unbuckled her seatbelt, opened the door, and climbed out. "Flies like a dream—an absolute *dream*. And it's so much fun to practice take off and landings on a real grass strip instead of a mile-long concrete runway. The left magneto is firing just fine now, Sam. You're a genius."

"Yes, I am," the man responded. "Handsome, too."

Jackie rolled her eyes. "One old woman smiles at him at the Lakeview Taco Hut, and suddenly he's Mister Macho."

Tina flopped down beside them on the log. "Well, as they say, spring is in the air."

Sam jumped to his feet and crossed his arms over his chest. "I don't have to sit here and have my love life ridiculed by my two supposedly good friends. That lady simply recognized quality when she saw it. And for your information, she gave me her phone number, and we're going out this Sunday night. So, excuse me for being both a genius *and* stunningly attractive." With that, Sam walked away, trying to look defiant and wounded at the same time.

Jackie and Tina laughed until their sides ached—their chuckles even bringing a smile to

Sam's face. When calm returned to the log, Tina turned to her companion. "So, what's up for you this week at school? Your teacher, Mrs. Maplewood, said that you're at the top of the class in everything but history. She said it broke her heart to have to give you only a B plus. Why, when I was your age, I'd be beside myself with joy to get anything better than a C."

"History is boring," Jackie moaned. "I'd rather study airplanes and navigation and air-to-ground communications. After all, I start flying lessons this summer, right?"

"Right," Tina said standing. "And if a B plus in history is the best you can do, I guess I can live with that."

"Well, it's not the *best* I can do."

"Hey, it's OK. A girl's got to know her limitations."

"I don't have limitations!" Jackie countered. "I can do anything I want, and if I want to get an A in history, I could—just like that." She snapped her fingers.

"Prove it."

"I will. Why, I'll—" She paused. "Wait a minute. Did you just make me promise to get an A in history?"

"Well," Tina said, "I believe I did."

Jackie pointed at her friend. "You're good, Dr. Taylor. You're very good."

Tina smiled. "Let's go in for some French fries and tomato soup before heading home to Oshkosh.

Last one to the kitchen is a tail dragger!" She began running in the direction of the hangar, her arms spread out like the wings of a bird in flight.

Jackie laughed and watched her go. Then she walked over and ran her hand along the wing of the Super Cub. "Being a tail dragger isn't so bad," she said, addressing the airplane. "It's the wings that keep you from falling to the ground—that take you high into the sky and carry you away. They are what's most important."

She glanced up at the clouds and studied their silky softness for a long moment. "Everybody needs wings," she said. "Everybody."

Jackie stood by the airplane, remembering her first encounter with the grassy strip and the man who called it home. Lifting her chin once more, she gazed into the vastness of the Wisconsin sky. "I love You, God," she whispered. "I love You."

Then she hurried away, eager to enjoy another meal with the two people God had waiting for her one dark autumn night when she fell.

# Airplane Modeling Honor Requirements

The requirements for the Airplane Modeling honor are as follows:

1. Build and successfully fly a rubber-band, or gas-powered airplane from a kit made of balsawood and tissue paper.

2. Build a balsawood glider from a kit, and observe its flying characteristics as related to the various positions of its wings.

3. Make and successfully fly two different styles of airplanes using sheets of paper between eight inches (20.3 cm) and fourteen inches (35.6 cm) in width and length.

4. Define, locate, and explain the usage of the following basic items:

a). Fuselage
b). Wing
c). Aileron
d). Rudder
e). Horizontal stabilizer

f). Strut
g). Cockpit
h). Engine
i). Landing gear
j). Propeller

**Book one: The Bandit of Benson Park**

Alex Timmons and his friends Shane and Alicia are determined to photograph a wild animal to earn their Photography honor. They set their sights on a squirrel in Benson Park, but capture a gun-wielding thief on film instead! Fear grips the quiet college town, and the photo puts the friends in danger. Read book one and find clues to help earn the Photography honor. 0-8163-1977-4. Paperback.

Boo

"Tl                              **DATE DUE**                    e on the
Wildern                                                          le plants
on a Pa                                                          ds themselves ri                                                        n an icy,
rushing                                                          arning a
Pathfin                                                          is! Book
two rev                                                          Honor.
0-8163-

Boo
Wh                                                               ions and
a strang                                                         Teaches
kids res                                                         Marine
Mamm:
0-8163-

Boo
Ale                                                              tery that
everyon                                                          Cooking
Honor                                                            ode that
proves                                                           he soup!
0-8163-

Eac                                                              ure that
demons                                                           thfinder
honor l
US$7.9

Or                                                               t online
and she                                                          com.

• R
• Order online
• Sign up for email notices on new products